To all the readers out there who demanded Gage's story immediately. This one's for you.

Torn

By Monica Murphy

The Billionaire Bachelors Club Series
Crave
Torn

New Adult
Second Chance Boyfriend
One Week Girlfriend

Torn

A BILLIONAIRE BACHELORS CLUB NOVEL

MONICA MURPHY

AVON IMPULSE
An Imprint of HarperCollins Publishers

Chapter One

Marina

"TELL ME YOUR name."

A shiver runs down my spine at the commanding, deep voice that sounds in my ear. I keep myself still, trying my best not to react considering we're surrounded by at least a hundred people, but oh, how I want to.

If I could, I'd throw myself into the arms of the man who's standing far too close to me. He's demanding to know my name as if I owe him some sort of favor, which I can't help but find hot.

Irritating, but hot.

"Tell me yours first," I murmur in return, turning my head in the opposite direction, so it appears I'm not even talking to him. He stands behind me, tall and broad, imposing in his immaculate black suit and crisp white shirt—the silvery tie he wears perfectly knotted at his throat.

I might not be looking at this very moment, but I'd memorized everything about him the moment I first saw him not an hour ago. He'd drawn plenty of attention without saying a word, striding into the room as if he owned it, casting that calculating gaze upon everyone in attendance. Looking very much like the mighty king observing his lowly subjects—until his eyes lit upon me.

He watched me for long, agonizing minutes. Butterflies fluttered in my stomach as I felt his hungry eyes rake over my body, and for a terrifying moment I wondered if he could see right through me. I shifted the slightest bit, inwardly cursing myself for coming tonight, but I held firm. I refused to react.

I still refuse to react.

"You don't know who I am?" He sounds amused at the notion, and I'm tempted to walk away without a word. My earlier nerves evaporate, replaced by a steely spine and an even steelier attitude. He's so confident, so arrogant, I'm sure he believes he has me.

He doesn't know who he's dealing with then, does he?

We're at a local wine- and brewery-tasting, and I'm here representing the bakery my family owns. The one I was recently allowed to take over and run since I'd graduated college. The business they all believe is going to fail. *So why not give it to Marina? She can't screw it up too badly.*

That's what I overheard my father telling my uncle. The memory of his words still cuts straight to the bone.

Finally I chance a glance at the man behind me, drinking in his thick brown hair tinged with gold, the way it tumbles across his forehead, his twinkling green eyes, the faint smile that curves his full lips. The combination gives him a boyish appearance. It's a complete illusion because there is nothing boyish about this virile man before me.

"Perhaps you can enlighten me." I offer a carefree smile and turn to face him, the nerves returning tenfold when he takes a step toward me, invading my personal space. His scent hits me first: clean and subtle, a mixture of soap and just . . . him. No cologne that I can detect.

Rather unusual. Most of the men I know slather themselves in expensive scents all with the purpose of drawing us silly women in. Instead, they end up choking us.

With the exception of this man. I find the uniqueness refreshing.

A slow smile appears, revealing perfectly straight white teeth. "Gage Emerson." He thrusts his hand toward me. "And you are . . .?"

He's not very subtle. And he's exactly who I suspected, not that I had any real doubt. The very man who recently bought up what feels like half of the Napa Valley, all in the hopes of turning it around and selling it to God knows who just to earn a hefty profit.

Not caring in the least that he's forever changing the landscape of the very place I've grown up in. And devastating my family in the process.

"Marina Knight," I say. God, I sound breathless, and I want to smack myself. I'm not here tonight because of him. I came for other reasons. To promote the family bakery, to mix and mingle with local business owners, many I consider friends. My life in the Napa Valley is all I know.

And this gorgeous man standing in front of me is trying to take what I know away from me for good.

His smile grows and a slow, burning anger—combined with hunger, which makes me angrier—threads its way through my veins. I inhale sharply, desperate to control the unwanted emotion. I knew he was handsome, charming, well spoken. I'd recently done my research; Googled him for a solid hour, trying to find any sort of weakness—since he certainly knows my family's—but it appears he has none. Like he's some sort of untouchable superhero.

I didn't expect my reaction to him, though. My body is humming in all the right places at his closeness. My skin literally tingles, and when he clasps my hand in his to shake it, my knees threaten to buckle.

"A pleasure to meet you, Marina Knight." His voice rumbles from somewhere deep in his chest and he draws his thumb across the top of my hand in the quickest caress before releasing it.

He's just a man, I remind myself. A dreamy, sexy man, in that polished, overtly masculine, deliciously commanding way that I don't normally find myself drawn to, but . . . hmm.

A girl is always allowed to change her mind.

"Lovely to meet you too," I say automatically, sounding just like my mother. Wincing, I look away, feeling foolish. I'm twenty-three years old. I've moved amongst the revered social circles in the Napa Valley all my life. My family is one of the most well known in the area. You'd think I'd know how to handle myself around charming, ruthless men.

But I don't know how to handle myself—at least around this one. Gage Emerson is intimidating. Gorgeous. Captivating.

I should run. Right now. Just turn tail and run. I don't know what I was thinking, hoping to talk to him. He's after my family's extensive property holdings throughout the valley. And I want something from him too.

The venue is small, at one of the many local wineries in the area. I'd found out Gage was coming so I planned to attend as well. I'd already talked to the winery owner, giving him my card in the hopes he would discuss the offer I made him earlier tonight, right before the party started.

The artisan breads my aunt bakes every morning would go perfectly with his wines. I've been trying this tactic for a while, approaching local businesses the bakery could pair with for promotional purposes, but so far, no luck. I'm starting to believe the word "failure" is tattooed on my forehead, and the only one who can't see it is me.

"Would you like a drink?" Gage asks. When I look at him once more he inclines his head to the side. "I'm headed to the bar. Care to join me?"

I follow him wordlessly through the crowd, murmuring hellos to the people I know as we pass, which is most of them. I've spent my entire life here. The towns that make up Napa Valley may be large, but the community is small, and everyone seems to know each other.

The gossip will probably be rampant with the fact that

I spent time in the company of the calculating, interloping real estate shark Gage Emerson, but I don't mind. Ultimately I'll get what I want.

Though he probably won't.

He settles his hand at the base of my spine, steering me toward the bar, and I feel his touch in the very depths of my soul. My knees weaken as we come to a stop, standing in a short line to order our drinks.

"So what brings you here this evening, Marina Knight?" he asks, making idle conversation. He doesn't sound overly flirtatious, but I can never be too sure. At least he's not touching me any longer. I don't know if I'd be able to form words with his hands on me. My brain seems to go into temporary lockdown just having him close.

"My family," I say, not wishing to give too much information away. If he can't figure out who I am after my introduction, then I really don't want to give him any more hints.

He lifts a dark brow. "Your family?"

"We own a few businesses in Napa Valley," I finally answer vaguely, stepping forward as the line moves.

He keeps pace with me, his gaze roving over my face, as if he's trying to figure out if we know each other. "Family businesses? Have we met before?"

I slowly shake my head. "Hmm, not that I can recall." I'd rather have him think he's utterly forgettable.

Not that he is. Oh no. It's only been a few minutes, but I'm afraid he's burned himself onto my brain forever.

"Huh." He sounds stumped. Looks it too. Which means he looks adorable.

His squeaky-clean image is the stuff of legend. Well, really his public image is one of all business, no play. Yes, he always has a beautiful woman on his arm at various public events. Yes, he's been linked to a few relationships, always with women who are as successful and powerful as he is.

So what could he see in little ol' me? The bakery manager with the giant family that's slowly losing its fortune, one buyout at a time?

Ugh, I need to push all the ugly thoughts out of the way and focus on the here and now. Like how can I convince him that the next acquisition on his agenda is off limits. The one he's going to be offering on very soon. The deal my family—specifically my father—won't be able to resist much longer.

I need to hold Gage off from making that purchase. He buys up the strip of businesses my family owns in St. Helena, and my career is over. My entire life I've wanted to run one of the family businesses, specifically the bakery. It was expected. The bakery had been a part of my life since I could remember. Now, with everything being sold off, there won't be any businesses left. After all that my family had done over the years, to be left with nothing makes me sick to my stomach.

I'm a part of the Molina family legacy, one of the oldest families in all the Napa Valley, yet I feel like there's nothing I can do. It's slipping out of my grasp right before my eyes and I'm powerless to stop it. Though maybe I could stall Gage for a little while . . .

But how can I hold him off? What can I do to stop him from changing my life forever?

You're a smart, strong woman. You can come up with something.

Sometimes I swear it feels like the voice inside my head is not my own.

It's our turn to order at the bar, and Gage asks for a beer while I order a glass of sparkling wine, locally produced. I'm ultraconscious of supporting our area businesses. After all, I'd hope for the same in regards to *my* business.

My failing business, thank you very much.

He pays for my drink, and I let him. He's still trying to figure out who I am; I can tell by his scrunched brows, his narrowed eyes. We move away from the bar but remain standing nearby. His back is facing everyone else still in line, and he's turned toward me while I'm leaning against the wall. He's got me effectively trapped, though I don't feel it. I rather like being surrounded by Gage Emerson.

Even though I shouldn't.

Gage

I CAN'T PLACE her, but I swear I've heard of her before. Maybe even met her though I can't recall where. Archer's hotel opening, maybe? I don't know. I met an endless stream of people at that specific event, though they weren't overly friendly. Most everyone in the Napa Valley still treats me like an outsider.

Marina Knight . . . it's her first name that's tripping me up. I don't know many *Marinas*. Or even one aside from her. Who does? But this one . . . she's beautiful. And not what I expected—though really? What the hell could I expect? I don't know her.

At least I don't think I do. And damn it, I'm too distracted by her pretty face. I think she's screwing with my brain.

All that calm, contained elegance she wears so eloquently is seductive. Honey-blonde hair that falls in gentle waves to the middle of her back. Cool, assessing blue eyes that seem to see right through me and are amused with what they find. Her mouth is slicked with a deep, ruby red lipstick and she presses her lips together before she flashes a mysterious little smile. Just looking at the gentle curve of them sets my blood on fire.

Not a good sign.

She's of average height, hitting me at about my shoulder, and she's wearing a simple black dress that covers her completely yet clings to every delicious curve. She screams both ice queen and touch me—an alluring combination I'm finding harder to resist the longer I'm in her company.

Lately, I've sworn off women completely. I enjoy spending time with them. I appreciate them like any other man. But they're a total distraction when I don't need one, always wanting more than I can give. Focusing on my business is the ultimate goal at the moment. Starting up a relationship with the potential for it to turn serious?

I don't think so.

Truly, that is the absolute last thing I want. Especially after witnessing my best friend Archer Bancroft fall hopelessly in love—with my little sister Ivy, for God's sake. I know that's not the path I'm ready to take.

Plus, there's a hell of a lot of money on the line. The asshole friend of ours who came up with the million-dollar bet, Matt DeLuca, is laughing hysterically at me right now. I can feel it; I can always feel it. I think he's here somewhere, probably spying on me as I talk to this woman I don't even know. All the while he's got that new assistant of his following him everywhere, sending him longing glances while he's an oblivious idiot.

She's got the hots for him, the poor thing.

We were at a friend's wedding when the three of us declared we never wanted to get married. We must've been drunk when we did it, but we all bet each other we'd never let ourselves get tied down to a woman. And the last single man wins one million dollars.

Fucking crazy.

If I have my way, Matt definitely won't win. Smug bastard. He thinks this situation we've all found ourselves in is hilarious. He believes he's got winning our stupid bet covered. Mister Lone Wolf has thrown himself completely into the renovation of the winery he recently bought. Women don't interest him, he told me just the other day. Maybe for a quick romp between the sheets, but nothing that could last. Nothing serious.

All the while, his very attractive assistant is sitting not ten feet away from us, her body stiff. I swear to God, her head tilted toward us so she could totally listen in on our conversation.

I'm with him one hundred percent in that regard. Let Archer take the fall—alone. He's thrilled to be playing house with my sister, which still blows my mind. Ivy's just as enamored with him. Funny, considering how not that long ago they argued all the damn time. I figured they hated each other.

Now ... hell, they're getting married in a couple of months. I'm going to be Archer's best man. Just thinking of wearing the imaginary noose that Archer's willingly walking into has me tugging at my suddenly too-tight shirt collar.

"So what brings *you* here tonight, Gage Emerson?" Marina repeats the question I asked her earlier, that same little mysterious smile curving her lips. There's a natural sultriness to this woman that calls to me. I can't explain it. I want to lean in closer to her and inhale her scent. Touch her soft cheek, take her hand and press my palm to hers. Something, anything to make that instant connection between us I'm suddenly looking for. Her lips drive me to distraction; they're such a lush, seductive red.

I bet she tastes fucking amazing.

Keep your head straight, asshole.

"Business," I answer firmly, sipping from my bottle of beer. It's from a local microbrewery that's become a recent favorite. That's why I came, that and—as always— to make business connections. Archer got me the invite. The more properties I buy in the area, the more inclined I am to stay here.

I like it. The countryside is beautiful, the people seemingly friendly until you want to take over their turf, and it's not too far from San Francisco, my home base.

I keep my eyes trained on Marina the entire time I drink, noticing how she jerks her gaze away from mine, her chest turning the faintest shade of pink, as if I might've made her uncomfortable.

Yep, I'm such a goner. And when I know I shouldn't be. I'm completely entranced. The women I'm normally drawn to are sophisticated, confident. My equals in age, status, and earning capability. I appreciate more of a powerhouse couple ethic. I sound like a complete jackass in my own damn brain, but I can't help it. I'm drawn to intelligent, confident women.

This one is young, pretty, and seemingly shy . . . with that air of innocent, yet sensual mystery that has me eager to get to know her better, despite my current aversion to the fairer sex.

"And what sort of business are you involved in?" I swear she just batted her eyelashes at me.

"Real estate." I take another drink, giving her the side eye as she casually averts her gaze, seeming to scan the crowd from over my shoulder. I glance behind me, seeing no one familiar in the room before I turn to face her once more. Of course, I'm the outsider here. And they're all watching me as if they expect me to grow five heads or something. I feel out of place.

Napa is small and everyone notices a new face. At least back home in San Francisco, it's pretty damn easy to get lost in the crowd when you want to. "I've recently made some purchases here in the area."

"Is that so?" Her lips curl into a knowing smile and I frown, trying my best to figure out who the hell she is.

But I don't know. Not for lack of trying.

"It is. There are a few more that I'm interested in too.

That's why I'm here. I'm hoping to find out some information."

She lifts an elegant dark blonde brow and my gaze is drawn to it. So she's a natural blonde? There's a rarity. "What sort of information?" she asks carefully.

"Well, I was hoping to run into someone from the Molina family." I've tried to contact many of them already, but they won't return my calls. "I know they still own a substantial amount of property and businesses in and around the area. And that they've slowly sold off a few pieces they felt didn't fit into their real estate portfolio over the years." I clamp my lips shut, afraid I might've revealed too much. What is it about this woman that makes me . . . forget?

Marina remains quiet for long, tension-heavy seconds. Pressing those sexy-as-hell lips together, she blows out a shuddery breath, her gaze narrowing. "So what you're saying is that you're a vulture."

Cocking my head, I frown. "What did you just call me?"

"You heard me. A *vulture*." Her voice drips with contempt. She scrunches her mouth into a sexy pout, her eyes coldly assessing. "You swoop in when someone is vulnerable and desperate for money. Then you take everything from them."

I never said any such thing, though she's right. The Molina family is vulnerable and looking to sell off their assets, considering they're land rich and cash poor. "I wouldn't call myself a vul—"

"No need to explain yourself." She holds up a hand,

stepping away from me. As if she needs the distance. The seductive smile, the sparkling interest in her pretty blue eyes, it's all gone. Doused like a flame under water. "I understand your type. It was nice meeting you."

My type? What the hell is she talking about? "Wait, Marina!" I call her name but she's already walking away, not once bothering to look back as she exits the building and disappears completely.

Chapter Two

Gage

"YOU DUMBASS, MARINA Knight is a Molina." Archer smacks the back of my head like he used to do when we were teens, and I let out a wimpy yelp, twisting out of his reach belatedly. Back then, I was usually quick enough to duck and miss that hard-as-hell-smack.

Now I kind of deserved it.

"I only just realized that. And trust me, I feel like a dumbass." I rubbed the back of my tense neck. Last night while lying in bed, I'd finally connected the dots and figured out who Marina Knight was. The last name Knight should've been my first clue. I did a little Google research, which enlightened me. Talk about feeling like a complete idiot.

I need a vacation. I can't remember the last time I've been able to let go and just relax.

We're at the restaurant inside Archer's hotel, Hush,

having lunch while I tell him what happened at last night's event. Archer was the one who'd given me the invite in the first place since he hadn't been able to attend. Too busy making kissy noises at my sister I guess. I don't remember his excuse.

So I went in his place. Sounds like I really stepped in it too. Something I never, ever do. I'm careful to a fault.

"A little late with that, aren't you? Her mother is Maribella Molina."

"I know," I interrupt, but Archer can't be stopped.

"She married Scott Knight back in the late seventies and it was considered a monumental merger of two of the most influential, wealthy families in the area. The Molinas and Knights are like royalty in the Napa Valley." Archer pauses.

That I let the Knight reference slip by shows how distracted Marina made me. I'm always on my game. I can always appreciate a beautiful woman, but when it comes to work, I don't let them distract me.

So what gives? Why is Marina the exception?

Yeah, Scott Knight might run everything, but all the businesses are still under the Molina name. Still. I'm irritated that I was such a dumbass.

A waitress stops at our table, refilling our water glasses before she flashes a flirtatious smile at Archer. He barely looks at her, offers a cordial thank you before she hurries away.

All the women love him, and he only has eyes for Ivy; thank God. I'd have to kick his ass if I caught him flirting with some random chick.

"Listen, I know who she is. Thanks for the explanation." All information I already knew. Though I can use it to my advantage. For whatever reason, it's been impossible to get to Scott Knight. And my usual tactics haven't been working. I can definitely put Marina into my arsenal.

That is if she'll ever speak to me again.

"Can't believe you had the nerve to talk about the Molinas in front of their *daughter*. You're a complete dickhead." Archer shakes his head, chuckling. "To be a fly on the wall . . ."

"Shut up." I sound vaguely whiny even to my own ears. I remember how she glared at me when I started talking about her family. *Holy shit*. So much disgust had filled her gaze. How she called me a vulture before fleeing, not once turning back to look at me despite my yelling her name. She'd hurried right out of that room as if the devil himself was chasing her.

Yeah. I really screwed that up.

"She's very close to her family," Archer goes on with a gleam in his eye. Like he's enjoying my misery by torturing me with more information. "I'm sure she's already run off to Daddy and told him everything."

"I don't need to feel any worse than I already do," I say, my voice low, as low as my mood. "And if that's the case, my chance at that strip of businesses in St. Helena is shot, huh."

"Yep, you're fucked," Archer agrees. A little too easily for my taste, but what can I say? I'm sure he's one hundred percent right.

I royally fucked this up.

Glancing around, I notice the restaurant is pretty empty. We're having a late lunch, and I should probably let Archer get back to work, but I'm frustrated with this entire situation.

"I don't get it. I don't know why I can't make this happen. It's like Scott Knight refuses to see me. I've tried to make an appointment with him multiple times. He never returns my calls." Or takes them either. If it was bad before, imagine how much he'll ignore me now after his daughter shreds my name and reputation?

"I'm surprised you didn't put two and two together, considering you've been hounding Scott Knight for weeks," Archer says, all nonchalant conversation-like.

My mind is spinning; I'm hoping like hell I can come up with a solution and smooth over this incredible blunder I've made.

I don't normally do this sort of thing—blunders. I'm efficient, conscientious, and, above all, careful. Archer is the screw-up. This is why we've always balanced each other out so well. He pushes me and I rein him in.

"You're always on top of your game," Archer continues. "What happened last night?" He contemplates me; I can feel his eyes staring at me hard. "You got the hots for Marina Knight, don't you?"

"Fuck no," I say way too defensively, glaring at him in return. "She's an ice queen."

"If so, she's a beautiful one." Archer lowers his voice. "Don't tell your sister I said that. She'd chop my balls off."

"Like I'd tell her," I mutter. "She'd probably chop *my* balls off by association. Marina distracted me. I took one look at her and it was like my brain froze."

"Ha." Archer shakes his head. "She has a bit of a reputation for being . . . indifferent. And for whatever reason, every guy who encounters all that cool indifference seems to get caught in that magnetic spell Marina casts. I don't know what it is about her."

Great. So it was nothing special between us. She's some sort of mythical siren. "I screwed up. I wish I could start over but it's too late now."

"You could go see her and apologize," Archer suggests.

"See her? Where?"

"She runs the organic bakery in St. Helena. You've heard of Autumn Harvest, right?"

Heard of it? That bakery is in the very block of stores I want to purchase. The Molinas had put it up for sale before, a few years ago, when the bottom fell out of the economy. They took it off the market before I could make an offer, not that I'd been in a position to make such an offer then. My money had been tied up in other properties and, just like everyone else in America, I'd been hit by the economic crash. Thank God I'd recuperated and am now doing better than ever. I'm a lucky bastard.

And, damn it, I want that property. The Molinas own four buildings on Main Street in St. Helena. Half of them need renovating, but they don't have the cash to invest in such major work. The lease was coming up on one of them. Another building sat empty. Revamping those locations would allow me to collect more rent money. And that money would make everything worth my while.

Though, I can't make the purchase if I can't get Scott Knight to talk to me.

"So it's really an organic bakery?" I ask. Sounds like a contradiction. I associate bakeries with sweet, sugary goodness, not good-for-you food.

"Well, they say that to please the health-conscious masses. And they make some delicious all-natural artisan breads. It's the cakes that kick ass though." Archer leans back, patting his stomach. "Ivy brought one home for my birthday. Best damn cake I ever ate."

"What kind? And does *she* bake them?" I found that hard to believe. She didn't seem like the sweet, domesticated type. Definitely doesn't look like a woman who likes to knead dough and frost cakes.

"She's not the baker, her aunt is. Marina manages the business."

Huh. Pulling my phone out of my jeans pocket, I bring up Autumn Harvest in St. Helena, clicking the "About Us" link. Impatiently I wait for the photos to load, sighing when I see the small pic of Marina Knight smiling at me.

This is where I recognize her from—the website. I'd looked at it before when I was gathering information. Ammo. Whatever you want to call it.

"I knew I recognized her from somewhere," I say as I stare at the picture on my phone.

She looks pretty. Accessible. She's wearing a T-shirt

that says AUTUMN HARVEST across the front. Her hair is pulled into a ponytail, her smile wide, cheeks a becoming, rosy pink, almost as pink as her sensuous lips.

I can't take my eyes off of her.

"I think you've got it bad for freaking Marina Knight," Archer said, sounding infinitely amused, the jackoff. "This is hilarious. Are you sitting there mooning over her picture?"

Clicking my phone off, I shove it back in my pocket. "No," I mutter, glancing about the restaurant. The place is now packed, and it's a Wednesday for Christ's sake. I need to change the subject and quick. "You must be making it hand over fist here."

"Business is good," he says modestly. "Brisk. This time of year is always better than others." He grins. "The autumn harvest is almost upon us, you know. The tourists come out in droves. Get it? Autumn. Harvest. You can't get away from her if you tried right now, bro."

Asshole. "You're real funny." I roll my eyes but he's kind of speaking the truth.

I can't get away from Marina Knight. She's invaded my thoughts the last few days. The last few nights. I regret pissing her off. I regret not getting to spend more time with her.

I also regret that she sounds somewhat like a man-eater according to Archer, though she hadn't given me that vibe when I was with her. Alluring, yes. Seductive, most definitely.

Sighing, I run my hand through my hair, glancing out the window at the gorgeous view of the vibrant green and gold vineyards in the distance. I need to make a gesture. Get on Marina's good side.

But how?

Marina

THE BOUQUET ARRIVED out of nowhere, a gorgeous burst of color, a variety of wildflowers in a giant glass vase with a raffia bow tied around the middle. The delivery guy carried it into the store with both hands curled around the vase, his head hidden behind the blooms.

"What the heck is that?" My aunt Gina stops right next to me behind the counter, her gaze wide, jaw hanging open. Her forehead has a streak of flour across it and the apron she wears is smeared with chocolate.

"I don't know," I answer as the flowers are set rather unceremoniously on our counter, directly in front of me. "They're beautiful though."

"And they're for a Marina Knight," the delivery guy announces, his tone bored as he chews his gum, contemplating me from around the flower arrangement. "Is that you?"

Curiosity fills me. "It is. Who are these from?"

He shrugs, not giving a crap. "I dunno. Check the card. See ya."

I watch him go, the glass door swinging closed behind him, the tinkling bell above the door announcing his departure. Aunt Gina nudges me in the ribs, her elbow extra pointy for some reason, and I grumble out an *ouch*.

"Check the envelope! I want to know who your new admirer is," she encourages eagerly.

"Hah, I have no admirers." And I like it that way. Men complicate everything. I need to focus on saving the family business, not worry if a guy thinks I'm pretty enough to ask out on a date.

Leaning forward, I breathe deep, inhaling the deliciously sweet floral scent. The flowers are so beautiful they almost don't look real. The arrangement appears haphazard, a casual gathering of gorgeous blooms, but as I look closer, I see that it's artfully arranged.

"They're lovely," Gina breathes, sniffing loudly. "And they smell divine. Even better than the chocolate cake baking in the oven."

She's right. I can't even smell the usual bakery scents anymore. All I can inhale is the fragrance of the flowers. Plucking through the arrangement, I run my finger first over a silky white petal, then a velvety purple one. I notice the pick nestled amongst the blooms holding a small, cream-colored envelope.

I tear it open and pull out the thick, square card, frowning at the sight of the unfamiliar, very bold script.

Marina—
> *I'm sorry. I hope you can forgive my rudeness the other night. Perhaps we can start over?*
> *Best,*
> *Gage*

Blowing out a harsh breath, I roll my eyes at no one. I'm freaking irritated he didn't sign his last name, believing he was that memorable.

And he had been.

A giddy, fizzy sensation washes over me, and I fight it down as best I can, but it's no use. I like that he did this. That he wanted to apologize by sending me flowers.

It meant he was thinking about me.

Taking a deep breath, I shake my head, focusing instead on why he had to make that apology in the first place. Talk about a grand gesture. The flowers had to have cost him an absolute fortune. Glancing at the back of the torn envelope, I see the name of the floral shop printed in tiny script in the upper left corner.

Oh yeah. I know they cost a fortune. Botanical is the premiere florist shop in the valley—and right down the street from the bakery.

"Who are they from?" Gina asks.

I glance up at her, sad I'm about to disappoint her. My mother's family has already written me off as a dried-up old maid, I know it. I'm freaking twenty-three but every Molina woman, including my mother and my aunt, were married by the age of twenty-one.

The way they act, they may as well set me up on the shelf and forget all about me.

"A man I met a few nights ago," I start, glaring at her when she begins squealing excitedly. She shuts up quick. "It was nothing. We were at that new winery's open house, remember the one I told you about? We started talking, and then he made me angry, so I stormed off. The flowers are his way of apologizing."

"Some apology," Gina says dryly, her gaze still lingering on the bouquet. "Why did you get so mad at him?"

"He insulted our family."

I knew that would get her riled. She stiffens her spine, her expression gone indignant. "What? How? What an insufferable—"

"I overreacted. He didn't know who I was." I shrug, trying to act like he didn't bother me too badly, but he so did. If I think about it too much, I could get angry all over again.

Angry and some other emotion I'd rather not focus on at the moment . . .

"He didn't know who you were? Who is this imbecile?" My aunt is outraged on my behalf. Gotta love her. "Everyone knows the Molinas!"

"First of all, I'm a Knight—" I start.

"And a Molina," she adds.

"Right." I nod. Proud Italians are the worst, as in the most stubborn people of all the land. At least my family is. "And he's not from the area."

My entire family tends to forget there's a whole other world outside of their Napa Valley glass bubble. As I child, I found it very secure. As an adult, I view them as narrow-minded and self-important. Sometimes.

Didn't you act a little self-important with a certain someone a few nights ago?

I frown. Really didn't need that reminder.

"Where's he from?" she huffs.

"I don't know. He didn't tell me. But I knew he was a stranger. I've never seen him before." I'm lying. Yes, he's a stranger, as in not local. But I know where he's from. I can't tell Gina I did a background check on him though.

Then she'd ask why, and I'd have to tell her, and I'm sorry, I don't have time to answer questions right now.

I need to work. It's all I do lately. I definitely don't get out much; the event where I saw Gage had been a social-working thing, so that doesn't count.

Otherwise, I'm so busy I'm either here at the bakery, helping out my parents, or having long meetings at the bank trying to straighten out our financial mess with an advisor who's worked for my dad since before I was born.

Then I go home late at night and collapse into bed, only to start all over again the next morning.

Talk about living in a sheltered little bubble. I'm the complete embodiment of it.

"Well. He sounds horrid." Gina sniffs.

I hold back from rolling my eyes. My mother's younger sister loves to rush to judgment. It's one of her finer qualities, my mom always says. Her steadfast loyalty is always appreciated. And we work well together, despite her occasional moodiness and uneven temperament.

Of course, she could probably say the same about me, so . . .

"He wasn't that bad." Major understatement. No, Gage Emerson definitely isn't horrid. Handsome, yes. Sexy, indeed he is. Confident to the point of smug, oh yeah.

I've always found confidence in a man attractive. I blame my father. He embodies all of those traits in a most handsome package.

"Do you forgive him?"

Blinking, I turn to find Gina studying me, her gaze shrewd. "What did you say?" I ask.

"What with the flowers and the card he sent you, do you now forgive this man who insulted our family? And why would he go so far and apologize like this? How long did you two talk?" she asks.

"I don't know. Ten minutes?"

Her lips tighten to the point of almost completely disappearing from her face. How does she do that? "So a man you spoke to for ten minutes and treated you rudely sends you flowers that probably cost hundreds of dollars? I smell a rat."

"You always do," I joke with her, trying to lighten the moment, but she won't have it.

Shaking her head, she rounds the counter and stands on the other side, sticking her face into the bouquet and breathing deep. "This is by far the most beautiful arrangement I've ever seen. And I've seen a lot." That was the truth, considering Gina used to create beautiful cakes for wedding receptions. We gave that up when I took over. I'd streamlined the business completely, something my aunt was very grateful for. She'd been working herself to the bone.

Now I guess it's my turn.

"He's just trying to impress me with his money," I joke, making her smile. "Probably hoping I'll fall to my knees and praise him for his lavish gifts."

"Now that sounds like an interesting scenario," a man's voice said from behind her.

Gasping at the sound of the faintly familiar, velvety deep voice, I glance up to find Gage Emerson himself standing in the middle of the bakery, looking disgustingly gorgeous, clad in another one of those perfect suits he owns. The man dresses to perfection. And why didn't I hear the bell ring over the door? "Oh my God," I whisper, absolutely mortified. His suggestive tone said he found my words . . . titillating. Great.

And while we're standing in the presence of my very overprotective and slightly angry aunt.

"I take it this is the rat?" she asks, making me groan inwardly.

"At your service, ma'am." Gage goes to her, his hand outstretched. Gina eyes it warily, as if it was a snake that might strike her at any moment. "Gage Emerson, aka The Rat."

She laughs and takes his hand, charmed. Just like that. It might not last, knowing my aunt, but come on . . . everyone seems to fall for him.

Why does her positive reaction rub me the wrong way? Why does *Gage* rub me the wrong way?

If I'm being honest with myself, I could get on board with him rubbing me the right way. And I don't normally fall for smug assholes. I'm attracted to confident men, but there's something about Gage I don't like. His arrogance is over the top. He seems like he'd be bad for me. And I've never had a bad-boy fetish.

Not that he's a bad boy, per se. But he's definitely trouble. Trouble I don't want.

Yeah, you do.

I'm arguing with my own self inside my head. Clearly, I've lost my mind. I don't get it. I don't get my reaction to him.

Correction. I don't want to react to him, and I can't seem to help myself.

Chapter Three

Gage

THE TWO WOMEN eye me carefully, the older woman—who I assume is Marina's aunt—relaxing somewhat.

At least someone has a sense of humor around here. You could cut the tension in this cute little European-style bakery with a cake knife.

"How are you, Marina?" I walk toward the counter, noting how she grips the edge so tight she's white-knuckling it. Do I make her that angry? Or maybe . . . that nervous?

I know she makes me nervous. She's all I think about, which can't be healthy.

For once, I really don't give a damn.

"Good." She lifts her chin, her expression neutral. Only her eyes give her away, a hint of nervousness fluttering in their depths. This woman standing before me is completely different from the one I first met a few nights ago.

This version looks younger, sweeter. More like the woman in the photo on the Autumn Harvest website. Not quite as poised as the elegant siren luring me in with her dangerous smile and sweet voice. "I'm surprised to see you here."

"My conscience wouldn't let me stay away. I had to seek you out and apologize for how I offended you." I gesture toward the flowers that cost me a shit-ton of money. Cost doesn't matter though, since I believe she's worth it. Getting me an in with her father, her entire family?

Even more worth it. Plus, I can eventually write off the expense.

Christ, you're a jackass.

I can't even admit to myself that I really wanted to buy her those flowers. That the bright, colorful arrangement made me think of her. Hiding behind it in the hopes of getting an in with her father is only part of the reason I'm here.

Marina Knight. She's the true reason I'm standing here worried I'm going to make a complete ass of myself.

"How did you find me?" she asks warily.

Now she probably thinks I'm a stalker. I can't give away my source. Yet. Archer's the guy I want to hook her with eventually. If I can't charm her, I need to find another way to make her see me again. "I figured out who you were and put it all together."

"Hmmm." That's her reply. She sounds like she doesn't believe me.

Great. I wouldn't believe me either.

"Do you like the flowers?" I ask when she still doesn't say anything else.

"They're beautiful," she admits grudgingly, making me smile. She doesn't return it, screws her lush mouth into a little scowl instead. "Thank you," she mumbles.

"So." I offer her my best, most humble smile in return. "Am I forgiven?"

"You think it's that easy, Rat Boy? That you can just waltz in here and have yourself declared forgiven all because you threw your credit card at the most expensive flower shop on this street and bought the biggest arrangement they've got?" Her aunt snorts and shakes her head. "I don't think so, young man."

Raising my brows, my gaze meets Marina's. Guess the aunt has no problem letting her opinion be known. "It was an honest mistake," I say. "And well, you sort of jumped to conclusions, you have to admit."

Marina's expression hardens in an instant. Jesus, what is with me constantly saying the wrong thing to this woman? I'm usually a smooth-talking motherfucker—direct quote from Archer—and if anyone is an expert at that subject, it's him. I put women at ease, I make them laugh, and if I'm lucky—on certain, especially rare occasions, at least lately—I get them to agree to come home with me.

"You're two seconds from getting kicked out of here," she whispers fiercely, her eyes shooting fire. Aimed right at me.

"Sorry! Shit." I throw my hands up in front of me defensively, her aunt's mutterings of "stupid Rat Boy" coming from somewhere behind not going unnoticed. "I just . . . I'm sorry."

Marina crosses her arms in front of her chest, the movement plumping up her breasts, drawing my attention. I can't help it, I'm a guy and she has nice ones. She's wearing a black T-shirt with AUTUMN HARVEST written across the front in elegant gold script, her long blonde hair pulled into a high ponytail, minimal if any makeup. She looks tired. There are dark smudges under her eyes and her mouth is tight. "Go on," she prompts.

Hell. I have to say more? Breaking out in a light sweat, I forge on. "I was rude. And I didn't mean to offend you. I had no idea who you were—"

The aunt makes a *harrumph* noise, but I ignore her.

"—and my friend had to point out who exactly you were a few days later." Stuffing my hands in my front pockets, I shuffle my feet, feeling all of about ten years old and having to confess everything I'd done wrong to my dad. Waiting for the inevitable punishment that was sure to come.

"Who's your friend?" she asks, her voice curious.

What? No 'you're forgiven,' or 'thanks for the apology'? I'm boggled. And I may as well reveal my secret source. I have the distinct feeling she's ready to tell me to get the hell out.

"Uh . . . Archer Bancroft."

Her arms drop to her sides, curiosity written all over her pretty face. "I know Archer. Vaguely. He owns the Hush and Crave hotels, right?"

Slowly I nod, wondering at the sudden gleam in her eyes.

"So how do *you* know him?" she asks.

"Where you going with this, girly?" her aunt pipes up.

"Gina. Don't you have a cake to check on?" Marina asks pointedly.

"Crap! I do. Oh my God, I hope it's not burning. I'll be back." Aunt Gina gives me the evil eye as she passes by and pushes through the door I can only assume leads to the kitchen, disappearing in an instant.

"Sorry about that," Marina says, taking a deep breath and exhaling loudly. "So do you mind telling me? How you know Archer Bancroft?"

Hmm. Someone wants something. I can see it in the way she's looking at me. Like her question shouldn't matter but it definitely does. I wonder what she wants from Archer? "We go way back," I drawl. This could be fun, making her work for it.

"Really? So are you two close?"

Best friends since high school, but like I'm going to give her that info. Yet. "Close enough," I say, purposefully vague.

"Hmm. You know, I had this idea I wanted to propose to him, and I keep forgetting to give him a call, I've been so busy. Maybe you can help me with that," she says hopefully, her eyes wide, her expression open.

Is she serious? I can't tell. But I haven't even earned her full forgiveness yet. "I can help you with whatever you want."

Her gaze narrows. "You say things like that, and it sounds sexual."

Guess this attraction between us isn't all one-sided. Good news. Just looking at her and I want to touch her.

Run my fingers through her hair. Drop a soft kiss to her very kissable mouth. She might punch me if I try though. Can't push her too hard. "I guess I can't help but think of sex when I'm near you."

Her mouth drops open. "Are you serious?"

Shit. Yep, there I went, pushing too hard like I can't help myself. I need to change the subject quick. Most women who flirt with me have no problem talking about sex. This one acts like I just asked her to commit a crime. "So, what sort of idea were you thinking?"

Her expression instantly goes blank. "Like I'm going to tell you anything. I don't even know you."

Fine. She wants to play that way? I can play right back. "You want my help talking to Archer?"

She nods so subtly I can almost believe she didn't do it. Almost.

"I need your forgiveness."

"You're forgiven," she says automatically.

Meh. That was quick. And it really didn't count since I know she didn't mean it, but I'll let it slide. "You can't make me feel guilty about this anymore. What's done is done."

"Fine. Great. Works for me." She releases another shaky breath. I think I make her uncomfortable. Perfect, because she makes me incredibly uncomfortable.

As in the *I want her so much I feel like I'm going to lose it if I don't touch her in the next five minutes* kind of uncomfortable.

"I'll need one more thing from you before I can make this happen," I say quietly, trying to amp the anticipation. I'm dying to see her reaction when I tell her.

Marina rolls her eyes, sexy despite her irritation with me. Since when have I ever been excited by a woman's irritation? I'm a sick bastard.

"Oh, come on. What more could you want?" She sounds completely put out. And clueless.

Well. I'm about to rock her world with one single word.

"You."

Marina

"LISTEN, I'M NOT some whore you can buy and sell," I say, immediately regretting my words. I sound completely over the top.

The look on his face shows he knows it. "That wasn't what I was implying," he says carefully. "I just . . . like you. I was hoping maybe we could see each other sometime."

The man is insane. Gorgeous and confident and with a surprisingly good sense of humor, considering how deftly he handled crazy Gina, but he's also a complete pain in my ass.

He has something I want though and I can't believe I forgot. Connections: one I somehow missed, so shame on me. And that connection is Archer Bancroft: a transplant, not necessarily considered a local, but definitely a man who's moved into the area within the last five years and done positive things to regenerate the economy. His hotel business is thriving; he's provided lots of jobs and plenty of sales revenue. He's solid, and his reputation is relatively golden, helped considerably since he settled down into a serious relationship. This community is small enough that everyone knows each other's business, and Archer's not shy about making a public statement.

He is definitely someone I want to do business with. I've had these new ideas bouncing around inside my brain, and I think he's the perfect candidate for one of them. Well, his hotel is the perfect candidate. If I could get my aunt's desserts into his restaurants, the extra exposure and revenue might help save the bakery.

And I exaggerated. I don't *know* Archer. I know *of* him. I've met him a few times. We always exchange polite hellos when we see each other at social events, but that's not very often considering I'm always working and rarely out. I just don't have time.

That's the extent of my so-called friendship with him. Whereas Gage really knows him. And even though I don't trust him and know he wants to buy up my family's property—including the bakery—I may as well use him while I can, right?

So yeah. I want him to get me an appointment so I can propose my idea to Archer.

Not with these sort of stipulations put on me though. Saying he wants me? That has cheap sexual thrill written all over it.

Sighing, I finally shake my head. "Of course. I know. It's just . . . it's been a long day. And then you send me the gorgeous flowers, and my Aunt Gina flipped out."

"She's quite the character," he inserts politely.

"You're too kind." Smiling wryly, I continue on. "Then you show up begging for forgiveness and . . . you distracted me."

"And that's a bad thing?"

"When a girl needs to focus on working, her business, and nothing else—yes. It's a very bad thing." Deciding to hell with it, I move away from behind the counter and head toward the front door, flipping the sign from OPEN to CLOSED and turning the lock.

"Closing up?" he asks. He sounds incredulous.

"There are no customers in here besides you." And it's near enough to our actual closing time that it won't make any difference.

"So are you going to answer me?" he asks, watching me move around the tiny café. His big body seems to eat up all the space, filling the air until all I can breathe and see is him. I do my best to avoid him, straightening chairs, picking up miscellaneous straw wrappers and crumpled napkins that still litter the tables. I'm trying to avoid answering him. Too full of nervous, restless energy he can no doubt pick up on.

What more could you want?

You.

I mean really. Who says that sort of thing? I feel like I'm in some bad, cheesy made-for-TV movie or something.

"What sort of answer are you looking for? You never really asked me a question," I finally say, glancing out the corner of my eye to see him approaching.

"I did so." He stops mere feet away from me. I can feel his body warmth reaching toward me and I'm tempted to lean in. Absorb all of that strength and warmth and gorgeousness. Though he looks utterly untouchable in the finely tailored suit that I can tell cost a fortune. "I asked if you wanted my help in getting you a chance to talk to Archer."

"Of course I do," I say, my voice quiet, my thoughts a confused jumble in my brain. What is going on here? Why am I even talking to him? Why do I want to be close to him? It makes no sense.

I can't stand him.

Really. I can't. I don't care how good he looks in that suit or how his sexy hair probably needs a trim. How bad I want to run my fingers through it. Or maybe grab his tie and yank him closer, see what he might do if I reared up on tiptoe and kissed him . . .

"Then go out to dinner with me," he suggests, his voice bold, his expression arrogant. The glint in his eyes, the curl of his lips . . . he's too damn confident. Like he knows I won't be able to resist him.

Irritating, because I'm this close to giving in and saying yes.

I slump my shoulders. Seconds ago I was imagining violently kissing him, and now I'm considering some other sort of violence toward him—like bodily harm. He infuriates me, yet he interests me. Usually if I'm interested in a guy, it's because I like him. I don't want to smack him upside the head.

"You're going to force me to go out to dinner with you and in return you'll help me arrange an appointment with Archer Bancroft?" I laugh though I find no humor in his suggestion. I might find it . . . arousing. Which is wrong on so many levels I lose count.

"I'm not forcing you to do anything, Marina," he says softly, his eyes glowing as they drink me in. "Unless . . . you like it that way."

Well, holy shit. The man needs duct tape wound around his mouth about twenty times. He says the worst things *ever*. "Did you really just say that?" I ask, my voice sounding deadly even to my own ears.

He seems to snap himself out of a trance. Standing straighter, he blinks, runs a hand along his jaw. God, his hands are big. I wonder what they might feel like on me. Sliding over my arms, my legs, between my thighs—

Get over it!

"Did I really just say what?" He looks dazed. The tension crackling between us has suddenly become unbearable and I have no idea why.

Um, maybe because you're attracted to him?

I push the pointless thought out of my head.

"Is it just me you say idiotic, sexist, disgusting things to, or do you talk this way to all the women you encounter?" I cross my arms in front of my chest again, noting—again—that his eyes drop right to my breasts. Men. They're all the same. And this one is so blatant, so cocky, and with such a rude mouth. He's downright offensive.

Yet my skin is buzzing just being in his presence. My blood is warm, my body both loose and anxious all at once. I only ever feel this way right before I'm going to have sex and I'm all amped up. Excited and nervous.

And I am never. *Ever*. Having sex with Gage Emerson. Oh hell, no.

A little groan escapes him and he closes his eyes for

the briefest moment, gripping the back of the chair directly in front of him. Damn, his eyelashes are thick. Of course. Everything about him is the epitome of male beauty.

He cracks his eyes open. "Did I really say that out loud?"

"Yep," I confirm, enjoying his absolute misery.

"I was thinking it," he admits, looking sheepish. Cutely sheepish. "That probably makes me a pig just the same, right?"

"Right." I nod, letting my arms drop by my sides. "I won't whore myself out on a date with you just to get a chance to talk to Archer. I can do that on my own."

A dark brow rises in challenge. "You really think so? Think about it. I'm offering you an easy in. He might throw up roadblocks, you know."

Knowing Gage, he'd probably ask Archer to throw up those roadblocks just so I'd go out with him. Jerk. "Oh my God. Are you implying I can't see Archer without you? Do you really need to be such an arrogant ass?" I toss back, immediately wishing I could clap my hand over my mouth. This man makes me say things I regret every single time.

"You're right." His vivid green eyes dim. "I'm an arrogant ass and I'm sorry. Forgive me again by coming with me on this date? I'll make it up to you."

I'll make it up to you.

There is a hint of sexual promise in his request, in that one specific sentence. I'm drawn to all that heady temptation, despite wanting to also knee him in the balls and tell him to go to hell. God, I hate rich dudes who think everyone owes them something. They are the absolute worst because usually, in the end, they always get what they want.

I've dealt with plenty in my lifetime. My family is both populated with and surrounded by wealthy, powerful men. We move in the same social circles. I went to high school and college with plenty of those who were going on to be successful, wealthy men—and women too, of course.

Except for me. My family is still drowning in a sea of debt, and it's only a matter of time until they decide to close the bakery once and for all. I think they believe it's a fun little project for my Aunt Gina and me. Like we're pretending to be business owners.

None of them understand how much this bakery means to Gina. Or me. I've only been running it for a year, but I've worked here off and on since I was a teen. It became my after-school job, my summer job . . . I met my first boyfriend here. Had my first kiss out in front of it, too.

Autumn Harvest has tremendous sentimental value to me. I also think it has tremendous potential, if only I could find the extra funds to make it really shine. Not that anyone cares.

"What do you say?" Gage's delicious rumble of a voice draws me from my thoughts and I blink up at him, still caught in hazy longing for the past. I make bad decisions when I'm feeling like this. All based on what my heart says versus my head.

My heart is almost always, always wrong.

"Say about what?" I ask, wanting to hear him ask me out on the dinner date again. I need to stall. I need to rationalize with my overexcited thoughts how going out with this guy is a huge mistake. My change of heart in regard to Gage is confusing even to me.

He smiles, the sight of it sending a flurry of butterflies fluttering in my stomach, and I stand up straighter. Determined not to act like a silly, simpering female.

I want to though. Just looking at him, listening to him talk, sets me on edge. In a deliciously scary way.

For whatever strange reason, I'm fairly positive Gage Emerson has set his sights on me. And I think I kind of like it.

His smile grows. God, he's pretty. "Go out with me. Come on, Marina. It'll just be a simple dinner, and in return you can have thirty minutes of Archer's time, or however long you need, to tell him all about this mysterious proposition."

"And what do you get out of this arrangement?" I ask warily.

"Why, the pleasure of your company of course," he says smoothly. Effortlessly.

Men who speak too effortlessly tend to scare the crap out of me. Usually means they're hiding something. My one long-term boyfriend in college was like this. Very charming . . . and eventually, he became toxic to my mental state. He was a liar and a manipulator. I don't need another one like that in my life.

So what is it about this guy that I'm drawn to? Because I am. I can't deny it.

I study Gage for a long moment, letting the anticipation roll through my veins. Saying yes would be tremendously easy. So would saying no. In fact, refusing him would be even easier. Then I'd never have to worry about Archer Bancroft or the good idea I want to bring to him. I wouldn't have to put on a phony show for Gage while going out on this date with him. Being something that I'm not; I do that constantly.

"Take a chance," Gage murmurs, his decadent tone reaching right into me, shaking me up. "Say yes, Marina. You know you want to."

"Hmm. Funny thing is I don't want to." I try to sound irritated and instead it comes out breathless. What is wrong with me?

His expression goes from confident to crestfallen, like I flipped a switch. "You hate me that much?"

"*Hate* is a pretty strong word, so let's just say I'm not your biggest fan."

"So you won't go to dinner with me."

I slowly shake my head, disappointment filling me, and I push it aside. I'm doing the right thing. I need to remember that. "You'll probably try to pull some funny business, and I'm a little behind on my self-defense classes."

"Funny business?" His lips twitch, despite his sadness just a second ago over my rejection. "You sound like your aunt."

"You're right. I do," I agree. "Going out to dinner with you would be a mistake, Gage. We both know this."

"We do?" He sounds surprised.

"*I* do. And I can't afford to make any more mistakes

in my life. I'd rather date no one than fall for some gorgeous guy who's out to manipulate me. Right?" I offer him a tentative smile, but he doesn't return it. I can't blame him. I just called him a mistake. We've insulted each other, lobbing them back and forth like a tennis ball for the last ten or fifteen minutes. Imagine an entire evening just the two of us? Tearing each other apart with our words. Maybe tearing off each other's clothes with anxious, eager hands . . .

Swallowing hard, I usher him out of the bakery with a few choice words and a firm push on his shoulders so he goes through the door. I slam it shut behind him, turning the lock with a forcible jerk. The loud click rings out—I know he heard it—and he glances over his shoulder at me one last lingering moment before he heads off into the sunset. As in for real, he walks toward the sunset, no doubt in search of his car.

Walking back toward the kitchen, my entire body begins to relax. I'm thankful to be out of Gage's presence. It's too overwhelming, just flat-out too much. He makes me think things, say things I don't normally ever think or say. I'm a nice person. I don't reject people or call them names. And I called him a disgusting pig. Talk about harsh.

What the heck is wrong with me?

Gage Emerson is what's wrong with you.

I barely hold back the snort of laughter. God, ain't that the truth?

Chapter Four

Marina

MY EYES BURN as I flip through the stack of bills yet again, pulling one out in particular that I've been avoiding for a while. I order flowers from a local florist—not the one Gage used because I *so* can't afford that place. Gina and I use them to decorate around the café where we can, knowing they add a nice touch. The customers appreciate them, as do Gina and I.

The flower order has gotten smaller and smaller over the last year. I'd started choosing the cheapest flowers they had, too. And now it's finally time for me to bite the bullet and cancel the order outright. I hate having to do it but we can't afford the expense. I'm trying my best to cut corners where I can.

And this is the next corner being cut.

Deciding I can piece out the bouquet Gage sent me and use the large variety of flowers for decoration over the next week or two if I stretch it right, I slap the bill on my newly made "call tomorrow" pile and sigh wearily.

Sometimes it feels like we're spinning our wheels. I'm doing everything I can to make this bakery work, but competition is stiff. There are popular bakeries and cafés all over the valley. The locals and the tourists love to get their eat and drink on so we're all battling against each other, trying to fulfill that need.

No one—and I mean no one—can make a cake like my aunt, but not enough people are discovering them or discovering our bakery. I got her out of the ruthless catering circle despite the loss of decent revenue. I had to do it. Baking and decorating elaborate wedding cakes every weekend was both exhausting her and killing her creativity. She does her best work when she can let the wild ideas fly.

Lately she's made some true masterpieces. They taste so delicious, and look so beautiful, it's almost a crime to carve into them. I have about a bazillion photos on my phone of her cakes, like I'm a proud mama dying to show them off. I need to create some sort of brochure featuring them all.

Another sigh leaves me, and I'm feeling stuck. We don't have enough money in our current advertising budget to do much beyond the chalk easel I set outside the front door every morning announcing our daily specials. We do a lunch special featuring sandwiches with our artisan breads and homemade soup that Gina also makes, so we get a terrific lunch crowd. Our morning crowd is okay too, but we're no Starbucks.

Grr. Just thinking of giant conglomerates makes me frustrated. Small towns gripe all the time about Walmart coming in and destroying local businesses. I'm starting to believe them one hundred percent. Walmart, Starbucks, they're all soul-sucking destroyers of the local business economy.

Yet I frequent our local Walmart at least once a month. Don't do Starbucks anymore, though. Why would I, considering I have an espresso machine here in the bakery and I know how to use it? Besides, I can't hand them four dollars plus for a coffee when my place is barely making it.

Propping my elbow on the edge of my desk, I rub my forehead, feeling the unmistakable tension there. I always get headaches when I pour over the bills. Who wouldn't, the task is so depressing. I press my fingertips into my skin in a circling motion, trying to ease the stress, but it's no use. The only thing that could cure my stress is a bottle of wine and a soak in my tub.

I remember my earlier encounter with Gage and glance over at the flowers sitting on top of the filing cabinet. I brought them in with me earlier when I knew I'd get stuck back here going over our bank account and the invoices due. If I'm going to do the drudgework then I need to make the spot pretty, right?

Plus, just looking at them makes me think of him. The things he said—both the good and the bad. And he says terrible things. It's like he doesn't even think. He's a successful businessman worth *billions*. Some of that is family money, but the guy is smart. Right? So how can he conduct business when every time he opens his mouth he says something crazy?

I can almost forget about the terrible things he's said when I think about how freaking gorgeous he is. How those beautiful green eyes seem to see right through me. Just one glance in my direction and he sets my skin on fire. Leaving me so hot I feel almost fevered every single time he looks at me.

And that his touch is my only relief . . .

Closing my eyes briefly, I stifle the moan that wants to escape and sit up straight, shuffling the stacks of bills into their own haphazard organized piles that only I understand. I drop them all into my desk drawer and shut it with a satisfying thud, then wipe my hands. Like I'm all efficient and totally handled yet another stressful workday, going over bills and taking care of business.

I so didn't handle it. I barely made a dent in our past-due situation. Yet another fun night trying to manage everything at the bakery, while it all falls down around me no matter what I try and do.

I push away from my desk and stand, then grab my sweater and purse hanging from the little coatrack I keep in the corner of the room. Hitting the light switch as I exit my office, I walk through the kitchen, smiling when I see everything shiny, bright, and clean. My aunt prides herself on keeping an immaculate kitchen and scrubs until it's spotless every single evening before she leaves.

Walking through the swinging door that opens onto the front of the café, I turn off the switch next to the doorframe, so the only thing left lit is the glass case that houses the cakes, cookies, bars, and all the other delicious stuff Gina bakes, though it stands empty now. Gina will be back at it tomorrow, arriving before the sun rises so she can make all of her delicious goodness ready for the morning crowd.

She can make a chocolate croissant that would have your eyes rolling into the back of your head it's so good. I'd put in a special request for them tomorrow just before she left. She said she'd make a double batch just for me.

Working at the bakery is going to kill my figure and make my butt big if I don't watch it. A girl can hold out for only so long.

I push in the rest of the chairs, the task forgotten after I rejected Gage and basically kicked him out of the café. Everything else in the area is clean. Perfect and ready for tomorrow—so why am I lingering? Shouldn't I want out of this place since I'm going to be right back and at it with gusto by seven o'clock tomorrow morning?

Where else do you have to go? Not like you have anyone to go to besides your parents, and they sure as heck don't count.

That is the most depressing thought ever. I feel like I've been listening to all the women in my family crying over how I'm a spinster at twenty-freaking-three and it's starting to take hold. If I think about it too much, I believe it. I'm a total screw-up.

Blowing out a harsh breath, I hang my head back, staring at the ceiling. Since when did I turn into such a world-class failure?

I hear a faint knocking on the front door, causing

the bell hanging above it to tinkle and I startle, looking straight through the glass and right at . . .

Gage Emerson? Standing on the doorstep?

I frown at him, wondering if I've become delusional. I'm hallucinating. No way is he really standing there . . . is he?

Shaking my head, I blink my eyes shut, counting to ten before popping them open again. He's still standing there, though now he's clearly impatient with me, if the glower on his face says anything. His hands are resting on his hips, pushing back his unbuttoned, elegantly cut navy jacket and showing off that broad chest of his, his tie loose around his neck, his shirt wrinkled. He's rumpled and looks absolutely delicious.

Oh God. I need to get rid of him, and quick.

Gage

MARINA IS LOOKING at me in utter disbelief. Like she can't believe I've somehow magically appeared in front of her. She even closed her eyes for a few seconds. Does she think I might be a figment of her imagination or something? I don't know. There's an entire building separating us and I want in. She didn't conjure me up.

Nope. I'm real. As in I'm the idiot who's drawn to her despite her obvious hate—or at the very least, disinterest in me. I must be a glutton for punishment because here I am, standing in front of her door in the hopes that just maybe she'll still be inside the bakery. Despite the fact it's past nine o'clock and she shut the place down at five.

Then unceremoniously kicked me out.

Luck's on my side tonight, I guess, finding her here.

Honestly, I don't know what possessed me. I left Autumn Harvest and went back to the house, hoping to get in a few phone calls. Hell, I even tried to call her father but he wasn't in. Not that he's ever in for me.

I think the guy is on to me. I haven't been sneaky about my approach, so I wouldn't be surprised if he knew all about my sniffing around his property.

But the thrill of the hunt couldn't hold its allure today. I got depressed. And I never get depressed. I've been rejected twice within an hour. First by Marina, then by her father. It's a multigenerational-rejection type of day.

Deciding the house was too quiet, and I didn't want to be alone, I left. Wandered down the cute little Main Street in St. Helena, purposely avoiding the bakery. I ended up at a bar and grill, where I ate dinner and consoled myself with a few beers. Watched the baseball playoffs on the flat screen TV over the bar. Giants were in the lead and eventually ended up winning the game.

The Giants are my favorite team. Hell, my friend Matt used to play for them, so of course I love them. But I couldn't work up even a trickle of enthusiasm for their win. All I could think about was . . . her.

She's consuming my thoughts. I never a let a woman do that to me, and I can't believe how fast my attraction for her has grown. I like everything about her, even how much she seems to hate me.

How driven she is, how protective she is of her family. I understand that side of her and I'm drawn to it, too. That she acts like she's attracted to me despite herself is intriguing too. Most women practically beg for my attention, drawn by my bank account more than anything else.

Not Marina. She'd rather I never darken her doorway again. And she'd most definitely benefit from my bank account. Yet she views my wealth with contempt.

I admire her for that. Hell, I want her more because of it. I feel like she sees me, the real man behind all the bullshit. Flaws and all, and despite that, the attraction is still there between us. Like a living, breathing thing. Does she see it?

If she does, she's pretending it doesn't exist.

A shiver moves through me as Marina slowly approaches the door, her expression wary, those pretty blue eyes narrowed as she studies me. I'm this close to leaving, but something keeps me there. I think I want to see what she might say to me. See if she's going to let me in.

I'm freaking desperate for her to let me in.

My problem? Too many beers made me think too much, and now here I am, basking in the bakery's autumnal finery. Late September and there are already a few pumpkins decorating the front. Two large planters flank either side of the door, filled to the brim with giant, rusty, orange-colored mums.

AUTUMN HARVEST is written in elegant black script across the door. The front window is large, allowing passersby a glimpse inside. Tiny tables and chairs fill the room. Large wicker baskets full of fresh fruit and wrapped baked goods line the walls. The bakery has a very warm, trendy Napa feel to it.

Yet she's having trouble with the business. I don't understand why.

Yeah. I really don't know what possessed me to come back here. I mulled over the reasons why Marina sent me packing for hours. I freaking still can't believe she told me no when I asked her to dinner. That she literally pushed me out of the bakery like she never wanted to see me again. I dangled the Archer carrot and she didn't give a shit.

She didn't think I was worth it.

No one tells me no. Well, I take that back. I've heard no plenty in my career. No is a part of negotiations. In fact, when I hear a no it makes me work that much harder to turn it into a yes.

But when it comes to women? They don't tell me no. I'm the one who usually turns them away. The one who has to break it off first. I'm not used to rejection.

Maybe that's why I'm drawn to her. She's the complete opposite of any woman I've ever met.

"What are you doing here?" she asks, barely cracking open the door. Like she might be afraid I'll push past her and force my way inside.

She wouldn't be too far off base. The idea does cross my mind.

"I don't know," I answer honestly, stuffing my hands in my pockets.

She studies me for a long, quiet moment and I stare back. She looks . . . weary. A little sad, a lot irritated. "I usually never stay this late," she admits. "Are you stalking me or what?"

"No, I'm not stalking you." I chuckle, shaking my head. A cool breeze washes over me, making me shiver, and I nod toward her. "Can you let me in?"

"I was just locking up for the night." She moves to close the door, and for a brief, terrifying moment, I'm afraid she's going to slam it completely and shut me out.

For good.

"Just a few minutes. I want . . . to ask you something." I made that up. I have nothing to ask her beyond *why do you hate me so much,* which has been running through my brain for the last five hours or so.

"Can't this wait until tomorrow?"

Jesus. I have never, ever met a woman so disinterested in me before. I hate it.

I'm more determined than ever to turn her no into a yes.

"No, it can't." I try to turn on the charm and flash her a smile, but even I can feel how halfhearted my effort is. "Come on, Marina. Throw me a bone here."

Rolling her eyes, she pulls the door open and I enter the quiet, dark bakery, brushing past her as I walk inside. I hear her sharp intake of breath when my body touches hers.

Just like that, I'm aware of her. Of every little sound she makes, the intoxicating scent of her, how she looks at me like she's ready to run and hide.

I make her nervous. Fuck, she makes me nervous. I shouldn't want this. Want her. She hates me. I don't like her much either. At least I don't like her attitude toward me or the way she treats me.

"What did you want to ask me, Gage?" She locks the door and leans against it, her tone bored, as is her expression. "It's late so make it snappy. I need to go home and collapse into bed."

Make it fucking *snappy*? I can't even acknowledge that or I'm gonna lose my shit and say something I really regret. And the bed reference sends all sorts of dirty images into my brain.

The fact that she's able to both turn me on and piss me off is quite the feat. She deserves a medal or something.

"Why won't you go to dinner with me?" I blurt, instantly hating myself for letting the question fly out of my mouth. I don't think I want to know her answer. I don't think she appreciates me asking when I sound like a whiny little baby either.

"You want the truth."

I nod furiously. "Hell yeah, I do."

"You're trouble." She says nothing else, just regards me with those cold, assessing blue eyes.

"I think you have me mistaken with Archer." No one has ever called me specifically trouble. Archer, yes, all the damn time. Me, Archer, and Matt together? Oh, hell yeah. We caused all sorts of trouble together, especially in our younger years.

But me, all alone? I'm not trouble. Not really. I'm a pretty responsible guy. My dad instilled it in me to take care of everything that matters. In business and in pleasure. When I see something I want, I go after it until I make it mine.

Is that what you're doing right now?

I push the scary-as-fuck thought right out of my head.

"I already told you I don't know Archer that well. I do know he has a reputation," she starts.

I interrupt her. "Well earned, let me tell you. He's an absolute dog."

"Hmm. Well, from what I've heard, he's settled down now that he has a fiancé."

My sister, but I don't bother telling her that. I have to keep some of my secrets. I might want to use them someday. And I can't keep up this pretense that Archer's a total dog because he's not. Everything Marina says is true. "Listen, I swear I'm not trouble. Trust me."

She laughs. "Any guy who says 'I swear' and 'trust me' is one hundred percent trouble."

I'm starting to get offended. More than anything, I'm fucking tired of dealing with her. Yet here I stand, still dealing with her. *Wanting* to fucking deal with her. And wanting to prove her wrong too. "You don't know me."

"I know your kind. You think you can get what you want and when you don't, you turn it into a challenge," she tosses at me.

Well, hell. She's pretty dead-on with that one.

"And I think for whatever sick and twisted reason, I've become a challenge to you," she continues, her eyes blazing with newfound anger. "I'm not some game to play and eventually win, Gage. I've already told you I'm not interested in you or your offer. What else do you want from me?"

I move toward her, grabbing her hand and pulling her to me. She presses her other hand on my chest, her eyes have gone wide as she stares up at me in shock. "I want a chance."

"If you're circling back to the dinner date thing, no. I think it's a bad idea." She takes a deep breath. "I think the two of us together is a bad idea. You don't like me. I don't like you. There's no point to this. We should walk away from each other right now."

Now that sounded dramatic. "I never said I didn't like you." I might've thought it because, hell, the woman loves to throw up roadblocks. I thread my fingers through hers, pulling her into me. Her hand is small, soft, and warm. I like the way it feels in my grip.

"We don't even know each other." Her lower lip trembles as she stares up at me. "You make me nervous, I hope you know."

"Guess what? You do the same thing to me."

She stares at me incredulously. "Really?"

I nod and don't say another word. Something about this woman makes me want to be honest with her. Lay it all on the line.

Whether it's good or bad. Whether I want to know her response or not, I need to hear it. For once in my life, I want to leave myself vulnerable when it comes to a woman. But only for this woman. She has me so twisted up in knots I don't know if I'll ever be able to unravel them.

I don't know if I want to either.

Chapter Five

Marina

WAIT . . . DID GAGE just say I made him nervous? Really? I find that hard to believe.

I'm so tired, so ready to go home and collapse into bed, yet here he is, holding my hand and overwhelming me with his mere presence. He's probably lying. Trying to get an in with me so he can get closer to my dad. Well, forget it. He can't trick me.

Glaring at him, I disengage my fingers from his, taking a step backward, but my butt comes into contact with the closed door, making me realize I'm . . .

Trapped. With Gage directly in front of me, looking all broody and handsome and grouchy and sexy.

I am so screwed.

"Stop trying to act like you're a normal guy with normal feelings," I toss out at him, wincing at how I sound like a sullen teenager. "No way do I make you nervous."

I mean really. He's a smooth-talking charmer. How can little ol' me make him nervous?

"You totally put me on edge. I don't get why you're so hell-bent on pushing me away." He stalks toward me, pinning me between the cool glass of the front door and his extremely warm, extremely hard body. "I can't figure you out."

"Maybe I don't want you to figure me out." I want him to leave before I do something really stupid.

Like let him kiss me.

"Ah, I think you do." Bending his head, he sets his mouth against my cheek, his lips whispering across my skin as he speaks. "Don't you feel it, Marina? Feel the chemistry between us, brewing and popping? Don't you want to do something about it?"

"No." Reaching out, I grab hold of his shirt, tugging him a little bit closer. Wait, what? I should be pushing him away. "This is a huge mistake."

"What is?" He settles those big hands of his on my waist. His long fingers span outward, gripping me tight, and I feel like I've become seized by some uncontrollable force, one I can't fight off no matter how hard I try.

That force would be Gage.

"I already told you." God, he's exasperating. It's like he doesn't even listen to a word I say. "Us. Together. There will never be an *us* or a *together*, got it?"

"Got it, boss." He's not really listening, I can tell. He's pulled slightly away so he can stare down at me, too enraptured with his hands on my body. A shock of brown hair tinged with gold tumbles down across his forehead and I resist the urge to reach out and push it away from his face.

Just barely.

He slides his hands around me until they settle at the small of my back, his fingertips barely grazing my backside. I'm wearing jeans, yet it's like I can feel his touch directly on my skin. Heat rushes over me, making my head spin, and I let go of a shaky exhalation.

"We shouldn't do this," I whisper, pressing my lips together when I feel his hands slide over my butt. Oh my God, his touch feels so good.

What the hell am I *thinking*? Letting him touch me like this? It's wrong. Us together is wrong.

So why does it feel so right?

"Do what?" His question sounds innocent enough, but his touch isn't. He pulls me into him so I can feel the unmistakable ridge of his erection pressing against my belly and a gasp escapes me. He's big. Thick. My thighs shake at the thought of him entering me.

I need to put a stop to this, and quick.

"I don't think we sh—"

Gage presses his index finger to my lips, silencing me. I stare up at him, entranced by the glow in his eyes, the way he stares at my mouth. Like he's a starving man dying to devour me.

Anticipation thrums through my veins. I should walk away now. Right now, before we take this any further. We're standing in the doorway of the bakery for God's sake. Anyone could see us, not that many people are roaming the downtown sidewalks at this time of night.

He's got one hand sprawled across my ass and he's tracing my lips with his finger like he wants to memorize the shape of them.

And I'm ... parting my lips so I can suck on his fingertip.

His eyes darken as he slips his finger deeper into my mouth. I close my lips around him, sucking, tasting his salty skin with a flick of my tongue. A rough, masculine sound rumbles from his chest as his hand falls away from my lips. He drifts his fingers down my chin, my neck, and my breath catches in my throat.

"Gage." I whisper his name, confused. Is it a plea for him to stop or for him to continue? I don't know. I don't know what I want from him.

"Scared?" he asks, his lids lifting so he can pin me with his gorgeous green eyes. They're glittering in the semidarkness, full of so much hunger, and my body responds, pulsating with need.

I try my best to offer a snide response but the truth comes out instead. "Terrified."

He lowers his head. I can feel his breath feather across my lips, and I part them in response, eager for his kiss. "That makes two of us," he whispers.

Just before he settles his mouth on mine.

The kiss is just the right blend of soft and hard, demanding and giving. I wind my arm around his neck, slide my hand into his hair and pull him closer. Needing him closer as our tongues dance, our sighs mingling together into one perfect, cohesive sound.

He pushes me against the cool glass, one hand still

gripping my butt, his other hand drifting down my front. A barely-there touch over the soft cotton of my T-shirt, my entire body tightens in response; my nipples harden beneath the lace of my bra.

I feel like I'm drowning. In his taste, his hands, his scent, his overwhelming presence. It's so confusing, what I'm feeling while in his arms. I don't like him. I don't want to want him.

But I do.

The kiss grows hungrier, more insistent. Our hands are everywhere, his slipping beneath my T-shirt to touch my belly. Mine slide down to curve over his very firm backside, squeezing, pulling him closer. Until we're nothing but a panting, yearning, straining mess.

I break the kiss first, staring up at him in dazed wonder. His swollen lips are parted, his hair a mess from my fingers, and he watches me, his breathing rough.

He looks too beautiful for words.

"We shouldn't—"

"I'm sorry—"

We start talking at the same time, his apology making me want to shove him away.

Instead I grab hold of his tie and pull him into me, our lips crashing together, our tongues circling, tasting. It's a frenzied, out-of-control mess, and I fall back against the glass door again, startled when I hear the familiar tinkling of the bell above us.

He ends the kiss this time, his gaze lifting, staring just beyond my head and through the door. "We need to—"

"Move this elsewhere?" I ask, earning a startled glance

from him. I bet he didn't expect that. "I agree." I push him away, and he steps back, looking just as dazed as I feel. Grabbing hold of his tie again, I take him with me, walking through the café toward the kitchen, the two of us completely silent.

I can hear him breathing, feel his warmth radiating toward me, and I let go of his tie, take hold of his hand instead. He follows behind willingly, his fingers locking around mine, and I hold my breath, afraid he might say something to ruin the moment.

Thank God he keeps his big mouth shut.

Excitement pulses through my veins. I can't believe I'm doing this. It's a mistake. I know it, and I'm sure he knows it too, but there's something about him I can't resist. The way he looks at me, the things he says, the way I feel when I'm in his arms, his mouth on mine, our tongues tangling . . .

He's irresistible. And I'm tired of fighting it. Fighting with him.

We enter the kitchen and the minute the door swings shut behind us, I turn toward him, wrapping my arms around his neck as he bends to kiss me. Our mouths cling perfectly, the taste of him becoming quickly addictive. I'm fast becoming addicted to the way he touches me, too. His hands race over me, too light, not lingering long enough, and I move against him with a whimper. His answering low moan vibrates against my lips, sending an echo through my entire body, and I shift closer. Restless. Wanting more.

I can't even question what's come over me. I don't kiss

men I don't really know. I definitely don't grope them either. I'm no prude, but I've never had something like this happen to me. It feels so random, so completely out of character. Scary and exhilarating and exciting and—

"You're thinking too much." He grabs hold of my hips and guides me backward, until I bump against the wall with a startled gasp. Taking my hands, he raises my arms above my head, pinning my wrists with his firm grip. "You need to learn how to just feel."

Before I can offer any sort of argument, he leans in to kiss me, softly at first. A teasing, gentle caress of his lips that makes me want more. His kiss slowly becomes harder, then hungrier, until I feel like I'm about to lose my mind—my very soul—to his greedy, wicked mouth.

God, he's so right. I need to forget everything and just lose myself in the moment. Lose myself in him. Let go of all my troubles, my hang-ups, my wariness over getting involved with Gage. I want to feel his hands. His mouth. His tongue, his fingers, his . . .

He breaks away to blaze a trail with his lips along my jaw, down my neck. My hands are still pinned in his grip, and I struggle against it, wanting to touch him.

Needing to touch him.

"If I let you go, are you going to run?" He breathes the question against my neck, his teeth nibbling the sensitive skin.

I shake my head. No way am I going to run away from this, though a tiny voice deep inside my mind tells me I absolutely should, that I'm about to make the biggest mistake of my life. "No."

His grip gentles on my wrists, his thumbs sweeping across my wildly beating pulse. I shiver at the contact, shocked at how he can illicit my body's response with the lightest of touches.

"I think I like having you trapped." He pushes my hands together and grabs hold of both of my wrists with one big hand, his other hand sliding down my front, between my breasts, one finger trailing down the center of my stomach to stop just at the waistband of my jeans, sending shivers cascading all over my skin.

"I'm sure you do," I say, trying for sarcastic, but yet again, I just sound breathless. Needy.

Damn it.

A smile curves his lips, the sight of it taking my breath away. "I'd like having you this way even more if you were naked."

Oh my God. I should tell him to go to hell right here, right now. We are so not doing this. Not doing it. Not doing it . . .

He slips his hand beneath the hem of my shirt, his fingers grazing my stomach, and I close my eyes, all protests, all thought forgotten. All I can do is lose myself in the sensation of his touch, the way his fingers curl around the waistband of my jeans before they move for the button. He undoes it easily, sliding down the zipper, brushing against the front of my panties, and I open my eyes, press my lips together to keep from crying out.

The jerk knows I'm holding back. His smile turns arrogant as he pushes first one side of my jeans down over my hips, then the other. He's surprisingly agile with one hand, considering he's still holding my wrists against the wall.

Not like I'd move them anyway. I sort of like being so open and vulnerable to his perusal. His touch.

God, why though? Why should I leave myself so open and vulnerable? Being with him makes me feel free. It's exhilarating in the most scary, forbidden way.

He's temptation personified and for once in my life, I want to completely give in to sin and not worry about the consequences.

"What are we doing?" I ask, my voice low. I need an answer. I need to hear that he's just as lost to this as I am. If he says the wrong thing, I should put an end to it right now. Kick him out and hope like crazy I never see him again.

Liar. You'd be devastated if you never saw him again.

He lifts his head, slipping a finger beneath the thin elastic waistband of my panties, touching the bare, sensitive skin of my stomach. I hold my breath, waiting for him to slip that finger lower, wanting it between my legs. "Do you have to ask?"

Smug bastard. "I don't like you," I remind him. Reminding myself, too. I really don't. He's trying to buy up my family's property so he can turn it for profit, and we'll be left with nothing but some cash in the bank, our legacy gone. I need to focus on that. How he wants to end our presence, how he wants to squash my secret dream.

But all I can do is savor his touch and want more. More, more, more.

"Good," he grunts. "I don't really like you either." All the while that finger trails lower, teasing down the front of me until he pulls completely away and out from beneath my underwear.

I feel the loss keenly, the bastard. "Don't—"

"Don't what?" He grins, leaning in to press his mouth to mine as he lets go of my wrists. "Don't touch you? Don't stop? Which is it, Marina?" He whispers the questions across my lips, his own hot and delicious. I'm torn. I don't know what to do. I want him to stop. But then again, I want him to keep going. I want to know what it feels like to be with Gage.

Feel him move inside me. Know what he looks like when he comes.

Closing my eyes, I fight my inner battle. And surrender myself to him.

Gage

SHE'S A GORGEOUS sight, pressed against the wall, her jeans hanging halfway down her thighs, wearing the most innocent yet sexy panties I think I've ever seen. They're white cotton, trimmed in delicate lace, the fabric so sheer I can see her pubic hair. A tiny white bow dots the center of the waistband, and the same silky ribbon ties around her hips, bows dotting either side of her.

I want to undo those bows and watch her panties fall away from her body. Then I want to get down on my knees and bury my mouth between her legs. I know she'll taste hot and wild. I wonder how many flicks of my tongue will make her come.

Fuck, I'm beyond eager to find out.

"Come here." She grabs hold of my tie—I think she likes doing that—and pulls me to her, my mouth falling onto hers. She opens for me easily, her tongue doing a wicked dance against mine that has me so hard I'm afraid I'll bust through the fabric of my pants, I want her so damn bad.

I guess the kiss is her answer to my earlier question. I know I shouldn't want this either. That if I think about it too much, I'll put a stop to the craziness. Because this is crazy, without a doubt. She's too prickly for me.

But the prickliness has all but evaporated, leaving a passionate, responsive woman in my arms. This woman shoving at my jacket until I shake it off blows my mind. What the fuck are we doing? We're going to have sex in the kitchen of her bakery. I've known her for only a couple of days. I'm trying to buy out her family because they're desperate for money.

And I'm trying to get in her pants because I'm desperate to be inside her.

She seems just as desperate, furiously attacking the buttons of my shirt before she yanks on my tie yet again, loosening it around my neck. I shrug out of it all then reach for her, pushing her shirt up and over her head, my mouth going dry when I see her breasts barely covered in the white, lacy bra.

Rosy pink nipples press against the lace as if they're yearning to be free. I reach for her, flicking open the front clasp. The cups spring away, revealing her full, perfect breasts, and I cup them in my palms, brushing the tips with my thumbs.

"Oh God." She thumps the back of her head against the wall, her eyes sliding closed as I continue to caress her breasts. I don't want to stop touching her, watching her, enjoying her. She's so damn responsive and I want to savor her, but my body—specifically my overeager and greedy-as-hell cock—has other plans.

Unable to resist, I lean in and suck a plump nipple into my mouth, lashing at it with my tongue, sucking hard. She threads her fingers into my hair, holding me to her, and I lift my eyes, watching her. My skin tightens in response at her expression. How lost she seems, how overwhelmed.

Fuck, I can't wait to see her pretty face when she comes.

Within seconds we're a flurry of hands and mouths. Clothes being shed until they form a big pile near our feet, shoes kicked off, condom retrieved from my wallet, until we're both naked and panting, grinding against each other but not necessarily doing anything about it.

Yet.

I pull away from her to tear open the condom wrapper then roll it on my aching cock. I can't wait to be inside her, can't wait to pound my way to orgasm and lose myself in her at least for a little while. Forget the battle and the angry words and the fact that I'm stealing away her heritage, just focus on the two of us together. Connected.

She whispers my name, and I glance up, find her staring at me with wide eyes and parted, swollen red lips. I go to her, kissing her soundly as I grab hold of her by the waist and lift her up. She weighs nothing; my hands grip her perfect ass as she winds her long, smooth legs around my middle, and I press her against the wall. My cock poised perfectly to thrust forward inside her.

"You're big." She breathes the words, my erection pressing against the soft give of her belly, and I smile, reaching toward her so I can brush stray tendrils of wavy damp hair away from her forehead. She closes her eyes and releases a shuddering breath, as if she has to prepare herself for this moment, and I'm suddenly worried.

Is she changing her mind? Ready to back out? Fuck, I'm about to enter her. If I think about it too long, I could probably come like an overeager teenager if I don't watch it. I want to make this good, I want to make it last, but not if she doesn't want this to happen . . .

"Now you're the one who's thinking too much," she whispers when I don't say anything, amusement filling her voice.

I meet her gaze to see she's smiling at me, the apprehension still lingering in her eyes, but I can't worry about it now. Carefully, so slowly I know I'm trying to kill myself by torture, I enter her body for the first time. I register the quick intake of her breath, the way her body tenses up for the briefest moment as I push inside. The give of her welcoming body as I go deeper, all that silky, hot wet flesh wrapping around me, sends me straight into oblivion.

Closing my eyes, I hold steady, my racing heart roaring in my ears. I press my forehead to hers and swallow hard, trying to keep my shit together, but it's so damn hard when she feels so damn good.

"Ohmigod." Her words run together as she shifts against me, sending me deeper and we both groan. "Move, Gage. Please."

I do as she asks, surprised at her request. Breathing deep, I pull almost all the way out, feeling her inner walls drag against my length before I plunge deep inside and she clings to me, a low moan sounding close to my ear. Her arms are around my neck, her face buried at the spot between my shoulder and throat. I can feel her lips move against my skin as she speaks.

"More," she encourages. "Harder, Gage. Please."

Christ. With that kind of encouragement I can have her bumping against the wall within seconds but I don't . . . want to hurt her.

My brain registers this weird realization and I pause, swamped with confusion. I always ensure the woman I'm with is satisfied, but I chase after my orgasm as quick as I can like any other guy. Guess that makes me a selfish prick. I think Marina might've even called me a selfish prick today, or at least a variation of it.

Somehow, now that I'm inside her, I don't want to be a selfish prick at all. I want to watch her, learn what she likes best. I want to see her eyes, her entire expression grow fevered as I continue to push and push with deliberate, sure strokes inside her body. I want to hear her breath catch, hear her whisper my name just before I make her completely fall apart.

And only then will I chase my orgasm. I want her satisfaction to come first.

I fill her, again and again, the slap of our damp bodies,

the sound of our sighs and moans mingling together. Reaching between us, I touch her; she's so drenched and hot. Circling her clit, rubbing it, I feel her tense all around me, squeezing me deep, and I close my eyes, hold my breath. Desperate to make myself last.

Desperate to make this so good for her she'll forget every man she's ever been with.

She's chanting nonsense. My name and *please* and other, unintelligible words mixed together, and all I can do is open my eyes and watch helplessly. Captivated by her expression, her breaths, the way she clings to me, her head tipped back as if she's lost in her own little pleasurable world. I move faster, grinding against her, waiting for her to fall completely apart because holy fuck, I'm dying to see it. Dying to feel it. Feel her.

And then she's coming, a filthy word falling from her lips as she shudders and shakes all around me. I remain still, my cock filling her, my thumb pressing against her clit until her tremors slow, and she becomes a warm, languid woman, limp in my arms, silly, sexy little words still coming from her lush lips in a breathy whisper.

Fuck, that is the biggest turn on ever.

Lacking control or finesse, I resume my pace and pound inside of her, intent on the orgasm that's barreling down upon me. I'm almost there, the familiar tingling starts at the base of my spine, and my thrusts become erratic. Pushing deep, deeper still, until I'm buried so far inside her I'm afraid I'll never find my way out.

Only until then am I coming, my body trembling, a loudly proclaimed *fuck* coming from deep within my chest as I come inside her. I clutch her close, bury my mouth against the soft, fragrant skin of her shoulder, and I bite her there, earning a whispered gasp from her for my efforts.

"Damn," I breathe as I turn into her, breathing against her neck. She smells amazing. Like sand and the ocean and flowers. Fragrant and so damn intoxicating I'm afraid I could stay like this forever, breathing her in, feeling her surround me.

"Um." She shoves at my chest and I lift my head away from her shoulder to find she's looking fairly awkward.

As in, *oh my God, I totally regret doing this* type of awkward.

Hell. I've gone and done it this time.

Withdrawing from her, she unwinds her legs from my hips. We're both silent as I set her on her feet, my gaze not meeting hers.

The moment went from hot to uncomfortable in a matter of minutes.

I watch out of the corner of my eye as she bends over and snatches her clothes up, and I do the same. We both get dressed, and when I throw away the used condom in the trash can nearby, I earn a snort that sounds suspiciously of disapproval coming from her direction.

Well, what the hell does she want from me? At least I used protection, right?

Fuck.

I turn to find she's completely covered though rather sloppily, her hair a haphazard mess around her head and her swollen lips still tempting me to kiss her.

By the look on her face though, I don't think she's in the mood for sweet kisses and a whispered, "That was fucking amazing."

"We shouldn't have done that," she blurts, clamping her lips shut the moment the words are out.

Ouch. I rub at my still bare chest since I haven't buttoned up my shirt yet. Well. That hurt like hell. "Too late," I say, because what else can I say? It is too late. We did it.

Best sex of my life and she's full of regret.

"It was a mistake," she continues, her words like daggers straight to my still wildly beating heart.

"Pretty bad for you then, huh?" I quickly do up all the buttons of my shirt, stuffing my tie into my front pocket. No way she didn't enjoy what just happened between us. "I couldn't tell, what with the way you screamed my name and kept begging me 'please'."

She glares at me. Great. We're right back at it again. "There you go, resuming the piggish qualities I find so endearing."

I shove my shoes on, not bothering with socks. I just want the hell out of here. My post-climatic high is fading fast. Hell, it's pretty much demolished. She's got me on the defensive, and I don't like it. "I think for once, we're in agreement," I tell her as I leave the kitchen.

Marina follows after me, her bare feet taking her pretty fast, since my angry strides have me at the front door in less than five seconds flat. "What do you mean?" she calls after me.

I turn and pin her with a glare, suddenly furious at her. More than anything, furious with myself. I hate how she's making me feel bad, like I did something wrong. Like we should've never had sex. Maybe she's not too far off the mark, but it's like she's rubbing it in. "You're right. It was a mistake. We should never have done that."

Turning away from her, I flick the lock undone and open the door, exiting the bakery without another word.

Chapter Six

Marina

IT TAKES EVERYTHING I have to get out of bed this morning. I hardly slept, my mind too occupied with last night's events. Every time I moved, trying to force myself to fall asleep, my entire body ached but not in a bad way. More in a *wow, that was amazing and I came so hard I almost blacked out* sort of way.

Not that I'd ever admit that to Gage.

What had been an amazing moment went south real quick. And it was all my fault.

Regret fills me at the way I spoke to him, how I called what happened between us a mistake. I mean, yeah. I sort of do regret that it happened but only because our 'relationship'—I have no idea what else to call it—is so bizarre. I don't know him, not really. And what I do know of him, I don't like. Every time we encounter one another, sparks fly, and usually they're angry ones.

Not last night, though. Those angry sparks turned into chemistry-filled sexy sparks, which then morphed into totally orgasmic sparks. God, the way he touched me, his mouth everywhere, his hands everywhere, his drugging kisses, his big cock moving inside me . . .

My body tingles just remembering it.

Forcing myself to get up, I take a quick shower, scrubbing my still-sensitive body carefully with soap. My palms brush over my nipples and they harden instantaneously. God, what would I do if he was in the shower with me? His big, soapy hands sliding all over my skin, reaching between my legs, his sure fingers touching me in that exact spot where I so desperately want him to touch. Bringing me to orgasm again and again—

"Marina! It's almost seven! You're going to be late!" Mom yells from the other side of my bathroom door, killing my delicious Gage-in-the-shower fantasy in an instant.

I really need to move out on my own, but I come from a traditional family and haven't really found the need to fight it. Until now.

Finally I get my butt to the bakery to find the pumpkins Gina had set out a few days ago gone, damp spots remaining where they'd been and a scattering of pumpkin seeds. I stride into the bakery and look around, waving at Eli, one of the two college students we have working for us part-time, on his perch behind the register.

"Where's Gina?" I ask as I get closer to the counter.

"Back in the kitchen. She's working on that second

batch of chocolate croissants for you." Eli grins and shakes his head.

I forgot all about the croissants. I think I'm still in a Gage-induced haze.

Entering the kitchen, I find Gina standing at the oven with her back to me, peering through the glass window to check on her croissants baking within. "Hey. What happened to the pumpkins outside?" I ask.

"Oh! You startled me." She whirls around, her smile rapidly replaced with a frown. "When I arrived this morning, they were destroyed. Smashed all over the sidewalk."

I frown in return. I stayed at least an hour after Gage left, mopping the floor, scrubbing down the wall he pinned me against. I'd been about to leave when I noticed the streaks all over the glass front door, from where he had me pinned there too. I'd had to grab the Windex and scrub 'til it shone.

Having sex in the freaking bakery was not the smartest thing to do. I still can't believe we did it. I mean really, what the hell was I thinking? He should be my sworn enemy, not the man who gave me the most intense orgasm of my life.

And if he ever knew that, I can only imagine the smug expression on his too-handsome face. The sight of it would probably make me want to punch him.

"I stayed pretty late last night," I finally say. "What time did you get here?"

"Around four. I came early, couldn't sleep." Gina opens the oven door and reaches inside, a baking mitt covering her hand as she slowly withdraws the cooking sheet from inside. Perfectly formed golden brown croissants fill the tray, the fragrant aroma making my mouth water.

And I left just past eleven, so it had to have happened between midnight and four. "I bet it was kids."

"I'm sure. I already cleaned up the mess. It wasn't that bad, but it makes me reluctant to set out any more pumpkins." Gina shakes her head. "Jerks."

"Yeah." Unable to resist, I pluck a piping hot croissant off the tray, tearing off a small piece and dropping it into my mouth. It melts on my tongue, warm and so freaking delicious I moan loudly. "So good, Gina."

She beams with pride. "Thank you. You know, you can check the security cameras. See if you can see anything."

"You're right." I tear off another piece and chew. I always forget about the security cameras. They're relatively new. "I think I'll go check it out."

"Let me know if you see anything," she calls after me as I leave the kitchen and head to my office.

Deciding I better check before I get on with my normal day and forget, I log into the security site we use, bringing up the outdoor camera. I fast forward through the film, not really seeing anything until around two-thirty in the morning, when two people with slender builds and hoodies over their heads and faces come along and smash the pumpkins against the sidewalk, kicking them over and jumping up and down on them like they're bouncing on a trampoline.

Yep, kids. So stupid.

They don't linger long and I stop checking, knowing there's not much I can do since I can't see their faces. Besides, maybe I could get them on vandalism charges, but come on, what cop is going to go after kids destroying pumpkins?

If it happens again, then I'll contact the police. For now, I'm letting it lie.

Huh. I wonder if the cameras caught Gage and me last night? My cheeks heat at the thought of seeing the two of us kissing in the front entrance, me plastered against the door . . .

Deciding to check the other cameras, I click quickly through the feeds, rewinding and fast-forwarding through the last few days, momentarily startled to notice that business is definitely picking up during the early lunch crowd. I usually don't come out and help behind the counter until around twelve thirty, but customers are coming in even earlier, the place looking packed around eleven thirty.

I know by the daily tallies that business is increasing, but seeing the evidence makes it even more real.

Great. Business is picking up, and I'm thrilled. But are Gage and I on the camera feed or what?

Continuing my search, my heart starts racing when I don't find any evidence of the two of us, when really there should be. The camera system cost a bundle when we initially purchased it, but the monthly maintenance fee isn't that bad and worth the expense. Though maybe I should reassess. Who really needs a camera on the kitchen? Really the only people who are in there are me and Gina and our handful of employees.

Right. And me and Gage last night . . .

Sitting up straight, I go to the kitchen camera feed, my head pounding as I scroll back to approximately ten o'clock last night. I start to fast-forward again, slower this time, until a horrified gasp escapes me.

Gage, with his back to the camera and still clad in his suit, his big hands holding my arms above my head as he kisses me senseless.

Arousal drips through me, slow as honey, and I lean my forearm on the edge of my desk. My mouth goes dry as I watch us. I feel like a voyeur even though I know it's me. And Gage. I can almost feel his lips on mine, our tongues touching, my hand buried in his hair—

"You have a phone call." Gina peeks her head around my office door, and I squeal, clicking out of the camera feed so quick I swear I strained my finger.

"Holy crap, you scared me." I rest my hand against my chest, feeling my rapidly beating heart. If she'd come inside, she probably would've seen the footage. How could I explain that?

And how the hell do I get rid of it?

"Didn't mean to." She lingers in the doorway, wiping her hands on her apron.

"Who is it?" I ask, breathing deep, smoothing a shaky hand over my hair as I try to gain some composure. Watching the video of Gage and me together has me rattled. And I didn't even really get to see anything.

I saw enough, though, to remember just how good he made me feel.

"I don't know. I happened to pick it up when I went

out to the front and he didn't leave a name. Just asked for you." Gina leaves without saying anything else, and I reach for the phone.

"Hello, this is Marina." The person on the other end is silent for so long I wonder if they've hung up. "Hello?"

"Hey," the word is breathed out, the voice undeniably familiar.

"Gage?" I tighten my fingers around the receiver, startled he's calling me. I thought he'd hate me, after what I did to him. "Um . . ."

"Yeah, this is awkward. Listen, I talked to Archer about you."

I'm stunned. Why would he still talk to Archer about me? "You did?"

"He's willing to meet with you sometime next week. He said for you to call his direct number at the office and you two can set up a meeting. You want the number?" Gage asks, sounding efficient. Very business as usual.

Nothing at all like the man who held me in his arms last night, murmuring filthy words in my ear while he pushed inside me so deep I thought I might splinter in two.

"Yes, I want it. Let me grab a pen." I find a notepad and pen and jot down the number Gage rattles off, his deep voice sending tingles sweeping over my suddenly too-hot skin.

Just hearing him talk on the phone and I'm a goner. This is so ridiculous.

"Why are you being so nice to me?" I ask, clutching the phone so tight I know my knuckles are white. "I—"

"Treated me like crap last night? Yes, you did." He pauses, as if struggling with whether he should say something or not, and I silently urge him to go ahead and just say it. I don't care what it is. I might get angry but . . . I doubt it.

Or the anger will just be rapidly chased by arousal, so hey, that works too, right?

The man has turned me into a sick, twisted woman.

I want to apologize to him for being such a bitch last night and kicking him out, but I just can't find it in me to say I'm sorry. And that makes me feel like an even bigger bitch. "I panicked," I say instead.

"Because we had sex in the kitchen of your bakery?"

Closing my eyes, I let my head fall to my desk, thumping my forehead on the thick pile of papers. "Yes," I agree weakly.

"I know. I did too."

He didn't seem panicked. He'd been really sweet and aggressive and sexy and gentle. I've never had sex against a wall in my life. I've never been touched, kissed, fucked—yes definitely never fucked—like that ever. Ever, ever, ever.

So it blows my mind that something so crazy, so absolutely, terrifyingly wonderful, happened with a man I don't really like.

You like him when he has his hands all over your body and his tongue in your mouth.

Lifting my head, I open my eyes and scowl, banishing the nasty little voice inside my head and focus instead on the man I'm talking to.

"I know you regret what happened, and I feel bad for pushing myself on you," he explains. "So I thought I'd call up Archer and get this handled for you. It's the least I can do."

I don't regret what happened. Well, maybe I do a little, but who regrets great sex? "You didn't really push yourself on me. And thank you," I whisper, feeling a little choked up because really, the man could've told me to fuck off and die and I wouldn't have blamed him. I would've deserved it.

"You're welcome." He pauses, again as if he's struggling with what to say next, and I get it. I feel the same way. "I'll uh, see you around."

Panic flares. I can't let him go. Not like this. "Wait a minute! Don't I, um . . . owe you dinner?"

He remains quiet, but I can hear him breathing. "You don't owe me anything, Marina."

I love the way he says my name, his deep voice seeming to caress every letter. Holy crap, do I have it bad for a man I don't like. "It's the least I can do," I murmur, throwing his words back at him. Maybe . . . maybe we can see each other again. One more time. It wouldn't hurt, right? And I need to make it up to him, how awful I was. How I basically forced him to leave.

We had amazing sex, and then we were almost angry over it. Like we resented each other or something. So weird.

I'm tired of feeling resentful. Can't we just . . . enjoy this connection?

"You're serious." He sounds incredulous. I'm not surprised.

"A deal's a deal, right?" Reaching for my mouse, I bring the security site back up, pleased to see I didn't exit completely out of it after all. The screen is right where I left it, me being held captive by Gage against the wall. I speed it up a bit, to the part where I can see we're completely naked. My legs are wound around his waist, my heels digging into his perfect, flexing ass as he pushes deep inside me.

I'm transfixed. Watching us having sex, having him on the phone, it's like Gage overload.

"You don't owe me this. I don't want you throwing this dinner back in my face like you're prone to do," he says grumpily. "Considering how you believe I always have ulterior motives."

I let the insult fly, too enamored with the sound of his voice while watching him hammer inside of me on the computer screen. I squirm in my seat, feeling like a complete pervert at, what, just after eight in the morning? "I won't throw it back in your face," I swear to him, not sure if I can really keep that promise. "I guess it all depends if you say something stupid to me. Like you're prone to do."

Ha. We sound like little kids fighting on the playground.

Thankfully, he ignores my dig as well. "I'm leaving for San Francisco tomorrow, so how about tonight?"

"Tonight?" I hit pause again on the screen and turn it off, turning away from my computer so I won't be distracted. "That's kind of last minute." Like I have any plans.

"I know. It's either that or we wait until early next week, when I get back."

I can't wait that long. I want to see him, which I sort of hate. I absolutely shouldn't want to do this. But my humming body more than wants to see him. "Fine. Tonight," I say curtly, wincing when I hear my tone so I try and soften it. "That sounds . . . fun."

He laughs. The jackass. "Yeah, you sound thrilled. Look I'm going to try and get Archer to accompany us. He can bring his fiancé."

"Wait, what? You want Archer to go to dinner with us?" Okay, I hadn't bargained on that. I'm going to have to be on my A-game if that happens. I might even have to present my proposition to him, and I'm not quite ready to discuss it yet. I still need to handle a few details.

"Yeah, Archer and his fiancé. Trust me, you'll love her. And Archer, too. This isn't some business dinner, Marina. Just pleasure."

Just pleasure. Oh, now those are two words that take on different meaning when used in reference to Gage and me.

"Okay." I swallow hard. "Let's go out to dinner with Archer and his fiancé." I close my eyes and push my desk chair into a circle. This is probably a really bad idea.

But I can't back out of it now, right?

Chapter Seven

Gage

"YOU WANT TO go on a double date with your sister and me?" Archer chuckles, the sound irritating as it rumbles in my ear, and I pull the phone away, wishing I could tell him never mind and hang up.

I can't though. Promised a certain someone it would happen, and now I have to come through on that promise. Plus, I want to see her again. If I'm lucky, maybe I'll get her naked, in a bed, where I can take my time and map her entire body with my lips.

Yeah. I can't get the thought of her out of my mind. The way she clung to me, the taste of her lips, the sounds she makes when she comes . . .

I tried calling her father first thing this morning. No dice. The man hates my guts or flat-out doesn't give a shit. So I need to get in his daughter's good graces and maybe eventually she'll introduce the two of us. It could be a win-win for everyone.

Because just as much as I'm attracted to Marina, I'm also attracted to the fact that she's a Molina. Scott Knight's freaking daughter. I am so close to getting an in with him, I can almost taste it. Does this make me an asshole, wanting to get closer to her so I can get to her father?

Yes.

Damn it. That's what I thought. And I hate that I feel this way, like I'm using her. Getting to know her, kissing her, having sex with her . . . it's changed everything. The power has shifted between us.

Not that I ever really believed I held the power when it came to Marina and me. She's been tough on me since the first moment we met.

And I like it.

"I definitely want to go out with you and Ivy tonight," I finally agree, keeping it simple, waiting for the inevitable questions.

"Who's the girl making you want a double date?"

There's question one. "Don't laugh at me," I start, but he answers for me, his tone smug.

"Let me guess." He pauses for dramatic effect. He's having way too much fun with this and the conversation has only just begun. "Marina Knight."

I don't bother responding for a few seconds. I don't need to. He knows he's irritating the shit out of me. When his chuckle grows into full-out laughter, I'm ready to end the call.

"How did you make that happen?" he finally asks when he gets his laughter under control.

Question number two. "I convinced her I was a good guy and now she wants to date me." Lies, all lies. Like I can tell him the truth.

I fucked her against a wall in her bakery. Hottest sex of my life. Dying to do it again.

"I call bullshit."

Well hell, now I'm offended. "Why do you find that so hard to believe?"

"You badmouthed her family. The Molinas and the Knights, they're all about the family. You breathe one bad word against them and they're ready to take you down and tear you apart. Every single one of them acts that way," Archer explains.

I remember her Aunt Gina calling me Rat Boy. That sounded rather . . . mobbish. Is that even a word? "You make them sound like the mob," I mutter, glancing about my temporary office. I'm staying at a house I purchased a few months ago in St. Helena. It's cute, small, and very old. Needs major renovations—we're talking a total overhaul—and I've been getting bids on the job over the last few days. Its central location makes it the ideal place to stay while I'm here in Napa.

"Rumor has it they might be, though I doubt it," Archer says, his tone serious.

"Mob ties, give me a break," I mutter, more than ready to change the subject. "Listen, she wants to talk to you." I'd fibbed a little when I called Marina. I'd left a message with Archer when I couldn't get a hold of him and grew too anxious waiting for him so I broke down and called her anyway.

I knew I could get him to see her, but I haven't confirmed anything yet. I just wanted to call her. Listen to her voice. Imagine the way she sounded last night when she whispered my name as I sunk particularly deep inside her tight, wet body—

"Talk to me about what?"

"Yeah, it's about business. She won't tell me what exactly, but Marina says she has a proposition for you and she kept meaning to call you but hasn't yet," I explain.

"Huh, wonder why she hasn't called. I've talked to her a few times. Nothing extensive though." He makes a noise; I can hear him shift in his chair, the unmistakable creak coming through loud and clear. "When do you want to go on this momentous double date?"

"Tonight? Maybe?" I wince, waiting for his answer.

"You gotta be kidding me. *Tonight*? You expect us to rearrange our schedules for you or what?" Archer sounds a little angry, mostly amused. His favorite thing to do is give me shit.

"I need to get in her good graces so she'll introduce me to her father," I explain. Well, that's part of it. I also just want to see her again. Want to talk to her, argue with her a little, until she gets that angry little shine in her eyes, and I become so tempted I lean over and kiss her.

"Really." Archer sounds doubtful.

"Yeah. Really. The guy has been giving me the complete shut-out for months. I'm dying to talk to him."

Negotiate with him. Make Scott Knight a deal he can't refuse.

"Ah, so there's the heart of the matter." Archer makes a tsking noise. "You're not trying to get in her pants. You're hoping to get in her dad's back pocket."

He's making me feel like shit and I refuse to. Besides, I've already gotten into her pants.

Yeah, you are such an asshole.

"You're not going to guilt me over this." I do that well enough on my own.

"Whatever. I understand. It's just business." Archer sighs heavily. "Let me talk to Ivy, but I think we can do this. I've got no major plans going on, and I don't think she does either."

"Thanks bro," I say. "I appreciate you doing this so last minute." I mean it.

"No problem. I've called you begging to help me out so many times, I've lost count," Archer jokes, though really, he's serious.

He's the one who usually needs to be bailed out, rescued, whatever. Our friendship has always had that balance. Archer's the fuckup; I'm the one who cleans up the aftermath. Or saves his ass.

Whichever is needed first.

Now look at me, running to him for favors. But that's what friends are for.

Ever since Archer started dating my sister, he's straightened out. It started sooner even, when he received the old Bancroft Hotel his father gave him. He immersed himself in his work, took it seriously and turned that crappy old hotel into the thriving, successful Hush—a premier hotel and spa.

Then he and Ivy started seeing each other seriously, and he really got his shit together. I hadn't approved. Hell, they kept their budding relationship from me for fear I wouldn't like it. I love Archer, he's my closest friend besides Matt. And of course, I love my little sister, and would protect her no matter what.

Archer and Ivy together though? The idea still blows my mind, and they've been a couple for a while now. Hell, he's so in love with her, he's going to marry her.

It's pretty amazing, seeing what the love of a good woman will do to a guy.

Not that I'm looking for anything like that—hell no. Not yet. I'm too damn busy to pay a needy woman any mind.

Fuck around with one, specifically one as hot as Marina? Yeah, I'm on board with that.

Here come my asshole tendencies again. Showing themselves front and center.

"Tell Ivy to not ask Marina a lot of questions, okay?" I request.

"What do you mean by that?"

"It's just . . . she'll be curious and want to know more about this woman I'm dating. And it's nothing. It's not really serious, on my part or Marina's part. I'm trying to talk to her dad. She's trying to talk to you. We're using each other," I explain, hoping like hell that's the truth. If Ivy and Marina start talking and become friends, that would be awful. I don't want to hurt Marina's feelings, but this has to be nothing serious for me.

Despite how amazing the sex had been between us, it can't matter. We're just having fun. Gaining something from each other. She has to know or at least assume I'm talking to her because of the connection with her dad. This makes me feel like an asshole because damn it, I like her. Despite her not liking me, I'm drawn to her like I can't help myself.

Because yeah, I'm pretty sure it's not serious for her. One night of sex. Tonight, just a dinner. A chance to speak to Archer and get to know him better. Hell, she can barely tolerate me. Most of the time, she provokes me enough that I end up making an ass of myself and saying something stupid to piss her off. Being with her doesn't bring out my finer qualities . . .

Except when I'm buried inside her and making her come. Then all is good in the world. All is right.

Yeah. We'll go to dinner, we'll both get what we want and then we're done. Nice and simple.

Just the way I like it.

Marina

"DARLING, WHAT IN the world are you doing?"

I poke my head out of my walk-in closet at the sound of my mom's horrified voice. She's standing in the middle of my bedroom, her eyes wide with shock as she takes in the disaster. My clothes are strewn everywhere. All over the floor, the bed, thrown over the chair that sits in the corner closest to the closet.

It's a pre-date war zone, and so far I'm losing the battle.

"Looking for something to wear." I get up off the floor and stand, wiping my hands on my thighs. "I have nothing."

She's still glancing about the room, checking out all the items of clothing lying everywhere, I'm sure. "I beg to differ. I had no idea you were hoarding that many clothes in your tiny closet."

Funny how it's my "tiny" closet. It's your standard-size master bedroom walk-in. Hers puts mine to shame. It's like an entire room, with an island in the center full of drawers where she organizes her bras and underwear. Lit racks line the wall, showing off her beautiful shoe and bag collections. My father had the closet rebuilt for her about twelve years ago. I remember being in total awe. I'd never seen anything like it.

Then I went on to have friends in high school whose mothers had even bigger closets than my mom. Talk about putting us to shame.

"Fine. I have nothing that I *like*," I stress, throwing my hands up in the air. "I need to go shopping."

"What for? Where are you going that you're so worried over how you look? You always dress so nicely, darling, except when you're working, but what can we expect? Not like you can dress up to dole out pastries and coffee." She smiles, completely oblivious to how she just completely insulted what I do for a living.

She does that all the time and it's irritating. Even a little hurtful, though I try to tell myself to get over it. But my mom has zero respect for my job or my business, and I don't understand why. I'm actually doing something with my life, but she doesn't even see it.

"I'm going out tonight."

"Oh?" Mom sounds casual but everything else about her demeanor perks up. Great. "And who are you going out with? Anyone we know?"

I really don't want to tell her where or with whom. She's going to jump to conclusions when she hears I'm going out with a guy and it's nothing like that.

"No one special. And no, I don't think you know him." I shrug, moving over to my dresser. Kneeling down, I tug open the bottom drawer and flip through my jeans, finally pulling out my absolute favorite. They're a dark rinse, skinny fit without being skintight, and they make my legs look long when they're really not. "No need to make a big deal about it."

"When you say things like that, darling, I'm assuming it's a big deal. You just don't want to get my hopes up." She clasps her hands together, her blue eyes that are just like mine twinkling with delight. "Is he handsome? How long have you been seeing him? What's his name?"

Look at her. She automatically assumes I've found a special someone—her word choice long, long ago, not mine. The twenty-three-year-old spinster is the disappointment of the family. It's ridiculous.

My friends definitely think it's ridiculous I still live at home, but that's the way it's done in a traditional Italian family. Usually. I'm the need-to-be-protected baby girl in my parents' eyes. Their only girl, since it's just my older brother and me. John is married with two babies, doing his own thing clear across the country in Boston, where his wife is from. They met in college, the perfect sort of romance that made my mom infinitely happy.

So now my parents focus all of their attention—much of it unwanted—on my lacking love life.

Realizing she's still waiting for a reply, I heft out a long sigh, glaring at her. "Mom. He's no one. I swear."

"Tell me his name," she demands.

"Gage Emerson." Just saying his name out loud makes my skin tingle. I love his name. I loved especially when I whispered it in his ear just before he came. Hard.

Taking a deep breath, I tell myself to calm down. Those are *so* not the thoughts I should be having with my mother in the same room.

Mom frowns, a little crease forming between her scrunched brows. "Hmm, I don't recognize the name. I don't know of any Emersons who live in the area, but I must confess, I'm woefully out of touch when it comes to those who are your age. I haven't been to the country club in forever."

She sounds so old fashioned sometimes, and what is she? In her early fifties? Mom acts and sounds much older. But she grew up in a much stricter world than I ever did. My grandparents wouldn't let her do anything.

It drives me crazy, how she loves to go on and on about me needing a man in my life. Her disappointment that I haven't found a boyfriend is her old-fashioned thinking rearing its ugly head.

"He's not from the area," I tell her, tossing my jeans onto the last spot of empty space on my bed.

"Oh? So how did you two meet?"

"At an event a few nights ago. Remember the brewery-and wine-tasting thing I told you about?"

"Ah, yes. So." She smiles. "What does he *do*?"

He's a shark who's sniffing around Molina property and wants to steal it from us for nothing so he can turn around and make a huge profit.

Oh yeah, and he's a sex god who had me screaming his name when he made me come.

"He's in real estate," I finally answer as I head back into my closet.

My stomach roils, and I press my lips together. Why am I going out with him again? Yes, I'm hoping he'll get me an in with Archer Bancroft so I can talk him into carrying Autumn Harvest bakery desserts at his restaurants in his two hotels.

I hope this entire setup works. More than anything, I hope I can enjoy my dinner tonight and not want to stab Gage in the chest with my fork. As long as he keep his mouth shut and looks pretty, we should be good.

You are such a bitch.

Maybe I am. But the man provokes me like none other. Both in a good and bad way.

Mom follows me, hovering at the open door. "Residential or commercial?"

I can practically hear her brain calculating how much he could possibly be worth. "I don't know. I'm guessing commercial."

"Ahh. That's nice. How old is he?"

"Um." I swallow hard. I don't know all the pertinent information about Gage Emerson beyond his name, that he and Archer are friends, and he's a jackass snake in the grass who's really good with his hands. And his mouth. And his . . .

Wow, isn't my opinion of him top notch?

"I think he's in his early thirties?" I wince, not one hundred percent sure my answer is right. Looks like Google and I need a second date tonight.

"Sounds like you don't know much about your young man."

I barely restrain from rolling my eyes. "He's not mine, Mom."

"Oh, someday he will be. If he's smart and realizes what a fine catch you are." She sounds so confident. I almost hate to disappoint her.

So I don't.

"He's very intelligent. I think he's fairly successful at his job." From the way he dressed and his arrogant attitude, I would say he's definitely doing all right. Plus, there was all that research I did on him. Not that I'm telling my mom anything. "He's handsome too."

Too handsome, is more like it. All that dark hair tinged with gold, the intense hazel eyes, rugged bone structure, and too tempting mouth—he's definitely gorgeous.

Not to mention that amazing body and big ol' . . . .

"He sounds delightful. Is he coming here to pick you up?" Mom asks, her expression beyond hopeful.

"I'm meeting him at the restaurant," I answer, ignoring her disappointment. I can't let it bother me. If I had Gage pick me up at the house, he'd get the third degree. My father would probably make him fill out a questionnaire to see if he's good enough to go out with me or not, and we'd end up here for hours. In the end, Gage would run screaming from my house, never to return.

And I wouldn't doubt for an instant that Gage is using me to get close to my father. Considering I'm using him to get an in with Archer, I guess I can't complain.

"I don't know if I like that," Mom murmurs, shaking her head.

I start going through my clothing again, pushing aside one hanger after another. "Let's see if this goes any further before I bring him around here, okay?"

"Of course." Mom nods but she still looks a little heartbroken. "I understand. Well, I'll let you get back to your search. Let me know if you need any help."

I watch her leave, jumping a little when she slams the door behind her.

I've disappointed her. Again. This time it hangs heavy over me. She makes me feel like a little kid. When am I ever going to do anything right in her eyes?

Exiting my closet, I grab my cell from my bedside table, shocked to see I have a text message from Gage. We exchanged phone numbers before we got off the phone earlier, but I didn't expect to hear from him.

How about I come pick you up tonight? Instead of meeting at the restaurant?

I frown. Did the man bug my room or what? It's like he heard the conversation between my mom and me.

I'd rather just meet you at the restaurant. It's easier, I reply.

He immediately answers.

It's no trouble. Really.

The guy doesn't quit. From what I can tell—and I barely know him—he's always determined to get what he wants. It's rather annoying. I need to nip this in the bud.

I'd rather you not meet my family. And I'd rather drive my own car.

There. Brutally honest might shut him up. Though I immediately feel guilty for sending such a bitchy text, I push the unwanted emotion aside. I need to remind myself he's a jerk who only wants one thing from me.

And it's not sex. He wants to make money off my family.

This time he takes a little longer to reply.

I have met your family. Your aunt . . . remember?

I let out a sigh. He fights just to fight, doesn't he? I think he likes going round and round.

Then meet me at the bakery at seven. Though I'll probably be alone. Gina leaves early.

I should make Gina stick around as the buffer. The last thing we need is to be at the bakery alone again. He might try and spread me naked across my desk and have his wicked way with me.

Lord help me, that sounds delicious.

I'll see you at the bakery at seven then.

Nothing else. No more trying to convince me to let him come to my house, no more nothing. I think I might've offended him.

I know I shouldn't care. I know it's pointless, but . . .

I feel bad.

Chapter Eight

Marina

"Hope your Boy Toy shows up soon. I'm about ready to take off," Gina mutters as she wipes her hands on a rag at the sink. She's just finished making a new creation, and I told her I'd wanted her to stick around for Gage's arrival so I could use her for protection.

She'd been surprised but hadn't made me explain myself too much, thank God. Just nodded, told me she was in the mood to experiment and since it was my Uncle Joe's poker night, she would stay after work and hang out with me.

So I watched her make a chocolate raspberry cake that smelled divine and had the best frosting I've ever tasted. All the while, we talked. About the bakery, what our individual plans were for the next year, what we thought we could to do take the bakery to a higher level.

It was fun. My aunt is savvy about business, creative,

with an endless list of ideas. I briefly explained how I was going to meet Archer. She thought it was a fabulous idea, which pleased me. I wanted her on board. I consider Gina my business partner, and I hope she feels the same way.

Plus, she helped ease my nerves about Gage coming to pick me up and take me to dinner. As the time draws closer to Gage showing up, I'm worrying about potentially bad situations. Like the two of us alone in his car on the way to the restaurant. Yeah, that could be scary.

Scary and exciting, if the two emotions can coexist.

I believe when it comes to Gage and me, they definitely can.

"Where's he at?" Gina asks, interrupting my thoughts. "It's almost quarter after seven."

I push down the threatening irritation, glancing down at my black sparkly top and picking off a piece of lint. I finally decided on a top that shows off a lot of skin without looking sluttish. Because I don't want to tempt Gage or give him the wrong message. I refuse to have sex with him again tonight.

And if he keeps me waiting much longer, we will most definitely not be having sex tonight. Or any other night.

"So he goes from Rat Boy to Boy Toy?" I ask her, wanting to change the focus of our conversation. If we keep going on about how late he is, I'm just going to get madder.

"Oh, yes." She smiles. "Rat Boy is quite handsome, so that's a bit of a stretch for a nickname, you know? He's got that pretty face I'm sure you enjoy staring at."

I feel my cheeks heat but don't say anything. I do enjoy looking at that pretty face. She knows me too well.

"And who wouldn't? I don't mind looking at it either." Her smile blossoms into a full-blown grin. "Has your mama met him yet?"

"God, no," I mutter. "She'd flip out and have us engaged within minutes."

Gina laughs. She knows it's true. "She'd probably be picking out your wedding china patterns and prepping the baby announcements."

I laugh with her. "She knows I'm going out to dinner with him, but I told her it was nothing serious. That it's just business."

"Business, huh?" You know, the more I think about it, I find it hard to believe. He's a charmer, that man. I think you might've fallen under his spell." Gina raises a skeptical eyebrow, but I ignore it.

"Really, Gina. This has nothing to do with his charm and everything to do with talking to Archer Bancroft about your desserts in his hotels. Remember?" When she nods reluctantly, I continue. "He's good friends with Archer. We're going out to dinner with him and his fiancé. I hope to present my idea in the next week or two, but tonight will help break the ice."

"Ah, such a wonderful idea. Truly." Gina takes off her dirty apron and tosses it into the laundry hamper, then comes toward me and wraps me into a big hug. "Such a smart girl you are, Marina. I wish your parents could see how much you love the bakery. I'm afraid they're going to sell it."

My heart sinks into my toes, reminding me of the other reason Gage is in my life. He plans on taking everything away from me anyway.

Makes me wonder why I'm trying to get in with Archer's hotels when the bakery might eventually disappear. "I wish they could see how much the bakery means to you, too."

Gina shrugs as she withdraws from my embrace. "Perhaps we should make a presentation to the family as well. Convince everyone that we need to keep the bakery for the both of us."

That sounds like an impossible feat. The bakery is right smack in the middle of the block of buildings that my family owns. I really doubt they'd sell all around it and let us have this space. "We can try, right?" I ask weakly.

She cups my cheek, giving my face a little shake. "Don't sound so defeated, girly. We could turn this around. Don't think we're already beat."

Hard to do, considering I feel like the both of us are working toward an impossible goal. "Yeah, I know." The bell above the front door jingles, indicating someone's entered the café. "I should go check who's here." It's probably Gage, and my heart starts racing just thinking about seeing him.

I have got it so bad. And it is so wrong to feel this way.

"Don't keep your new man waiting," Gina teases and I stick my tongue out at her.

Someone clears their throat, drawing mine and Gina's

attention. We both turn toward the front of the kitchen to find Gage standing in the doorway, looking downright sinful clad in jeans and a charcoal-gray sweater. He smiles at us, but I see the apprehension in his eyes.

He looks nervous. I think it's cute. Plus, his discomfort eases mine.

"Well, look who finally decided to show up," Gina declares in her booming voice as she moves away from me. She strides toward Gage, grabs him by his broad shoulders, and pulls him into an easy hug.

He looks startled, patting her back awkwardly. "Nice to see you again, Aunt Gina."

"Great to see you, too. You do casual very well." She pats his chest, her fingers lingering.

Oh, good lord. Talk about embarrassing. And are his cheeks turning pink?

"Look at him, Marina. Your Boy Toy is extra pretty tonight." Gina takes Gage by the hand and leads him to me.

"Boy Toy?" He raises a brow, stopping just in front of me. His full lips are curved into a secretive smile and a rush of memories floods me. How those lips feel on mine. How excellent he is with his hands. The smell of his skin, the way his soft hair curls around my fingers . . .

"I've upgraded your nickname. Thought Rat Boy was a little rude," Gina explains.

His expression goes solemn, though his lips twitch. "I appreciate that."

"Well, you two best be moving along. You've kept Marina here waiting long enough." She pushes the both of us, hurrying us out of the kitchen. I grab my purse from where I left it beneath the front counter, slinging it over my shoulder as I watch Gina bustle around the café, checking everything before locking up. "You two have fun tonight, all right?"

"Need any help?" I ask, keeping my voice low when I grab hold of her elbow before she can escape me again.

She flashes me a smile. "I've got this, sweetheart. You go have fun."

I release my hold on her, rolling my eyes as I turn to Gage. He's watching me; his gaze sweeps over me, slow and easy, and just like that arousal trickles through my blood, heating my skin. My aunt is forgotten, the bakery, everything else, and it's just me and him, standing in front of the door, the spot where just last night he had me pressed against the cold glass while he kissed me senseless.

"So I'm your Boy Toy?" he asks, his voice a husky murmur that sends chills down my spine.

"If the shoe fits," I tease, pleased when he opens the door for me like a gentleman should. He has manners. This is a plus.

"I have no problem with it," he teases back, his eyes twinkling. "I know you weren't complaining last night."

Glaring at him, I tilt my head to my thankfully still oblivious aunt. "Keep your voice down."

His expression switches to serious. "Sorry. Forgot myself."

I understand. I think we both forget ourselves when

we're in each other's presence. Easy to do, considering the obvious chemistry sparkling between us.

This is going to be a long night.

Gage

SHE'S SO FUCKING gorgeous I can't get over it. All that long, tumbling blonde hair caught up in a high ponytail, showing off the pretty, irresistible curve of her neck. The neck I licked and nibbled last night, making her groan with pleasure, her hands clutching me tight . . .

Blowing out a harsh breath, I lead her outside toward where my car is parked at the curb. She stops short when she sees it, her wide-eyed gaze meeting mine. "That's your car?"

I nod, hitting the keyless remote in my hand so the doors unlock. "Yeah, that's my baby." I open the door to my newest purchase—a sleek, pearl-white Maserati Ghibli—and as I guide her into her seat, I can't help but like the way she looks settled inside my car.

I like the way she looks everywhere, as long as she's with me, if I'm being truthful.

What the ever-loving fuck?

Yeah. I've lost my mind. One night with a woman and I'm addicted. I think I want her even more because she's so damn indifferent.

"Your baby?" she asks me pointedly when I slide into the driver's seat, gripping the steering wheel. "This is a Ghibli."

Okay. I'm fucking impressed. Most women don't give a shit about cars. Or they'll be able to recognize a brand but not the model. "You're right. I have a thing for cars. I like to collect them," I admit, starting the vehicle. It roars to life, the engine purring a low, sexy rumble that seems to vibrate throughout the entire interior.

I wonder if Marina would let me bang her in the back seat. That would make this a more than memorable date.

"I love Maserati. My dad has owned a few himself. He used to collect cars," she admits, her voice wistful. "Not so much the last few years since he really doesn't have the time. Or the money."

Guilt assuages me at the money reference. But I can't help but be excited by the discovery that I have something in common with Scott Knight. "How many cars does he have?"

"Too many for me to count." She laughs and shakes her head, her hair rubbing against the soft Italian cream-colored leather. "He had an entire shop built to store them all. Most of them are vintage American classics mixed with a few Italian vehicles—homage to my mother's family."

"Nice." I pull out into traffic, shifting the car into gear as I slow down, and turn right. "I have a garage filled with the cars I've collected over the years. I started collecting when I was twenty-one."

"Really? How many do you have?"

I'm sort of blown away that we're having a normal conversation like normal people. No snarky remarks or rude comments. And that we actually have something in common—it's one of my favorite things to talk about, fast and expensive cars. "I have some in storage too. I think—

yeah, I have close to one hundred cars in my collection so far."

"Wow. I know my dad had more than one hundred at one point, but I'm afraid he's sold quite a few of them." She nibbles on her lower lip, looking worried. "It makes him sad to lose them, but it needed to be done."

I can't imagine having to sell even one of my cars because times were tough. I'd do it if I had to but . . . I wouldn't want to. I feel for her father.

I also feel like an asshole. I want to buy property from her father for a steal, so I can turn it around and make a profit. Plus, I'm dating his daughter in the hopes I can get closer to him.

Though, really I like her. A lot. I'm not with her just so I can have an in with Scott Knight. I'm with Marina because I want to be.

"I'd love to see what remains of his collection some time." I would. Not just because I could get an in with him, but I'm genuinely interested. What if he has my dream car in his shop? Not that I have a particular car I'm yearning for, but hey, it could happen.

"Um, yeah." She fidgets in her seat, looking decidedly uncomfortable. "You know I still live at home, right?"

I'm shocked. I hadn't a clue. "You do? How old are you?"

She glares at me. Uh oh. Here we go, right into "let's-see-how-out-of-hand-we-can-get-before-we-start-calling-each-other-names." "I'm twenty-three," she sniffs, all haughty Italian princess-like. "How old are you?"

"Twenty-eight."

"Really?" She sounds surprised. I glance at her to find she looks surprised too. "I thought you were older."

"How much older?" Shit, do I look old? I'm tempted to check myself out in the rearview mirror, but I resist the urge.

"I don't know." She shrugs, glances out the window. "Early thirties?"

"You like older men?" I tease.

She turns to glare at me again. "Not at all. I usually date men more *my* age." Her comment is pointed. Now she's really making me feel like a dirty, lecherous old man.

"I'm not even thirty," I mutter, shaking my head. Maybe we should quit talking. I never know what's going on in Marina's head. Our banter feels pretty comfortable at the moment, but we could slip into argument mode in a hot second. And I don't want us fighting before we get to the restaurant. Ivy will pick up on the tension rumbling between us and want to know what's going on. So would Archer probably, though he's pretty damn oblivious when it comes to that stuff.

Marina remains quiet, too; her hands curled in her lap, her head turned away, so she can stare out the window and watch the passing scenery. So I remain silent, sneaking the occasional glance at her hair, loving the multiple shades of blonde and brown mixed, knowing without a doubt that she's a natural blonde, now that I've seen her naked.

Thinking of her naked sends my thoughts into other directions. Dangerous, dirty, and unnecessary directions that I shouldn't be focusing on at the moment. Thinking of the two of us together leaves me feeling needy. Vulnerable.

Hungry. Starving, more like it. All for her.

Fuck.

"Can I ask you a question?" I gotta break the tension and talk about something else before I lose it and attack her.

She turns to look at me. "Go for it," she says warily.

"You're a blonde."

A smile teases the corner of her lips. "That's not a question."

"I thought Italians weren't normally blonde," I say lamely, feeling like a jackass. I'm trying to make conversation, and I feel like an idiot. This woman just makes me so damn . . . nervous. I can't explain it.

"I'm not one hundred percent Italian, you know. My dad is what he calls a mutt," she says, her voice light. She seems to like talking about her family, and I like it too. Any tidbit I can get on Scott Knight, I can turn around and use later.

But I also like learning more about her. I'm curious. I want to know. Usually I run the other direction when a woman wants to tell me her life story. So many of them do, going on and on about their past, their family, their friends. It all starts to sound like monotonous noise after a while.

Not with this woman. She offers these glimpses of her personal life so rarely, I cherish every tidbit I learn. Which is fucking crazy, truly. I shouldn't be that wrapped up in her, wanting to learn more, everything about her, wanting to kiss her . . .

"A mutt, huh?" I don't even know what to say to that for fear I'll mistakenly insult her father and piss her off.

She offers me a secretive smile, the sight of it sending a zing straight to my heart—and my cock. This woman twists me up into such complete knots, I don't know if I'll ever be able to unwind myself from them—or her. "My mother is Sicilian. There are a lot of blonde, blue- and green-eyed Sicilians out there. I happen to be one of them."

A beautiful one, too. She's so beautiful just looking at her hurts.

Not having her in front of me to look at hurts too.

Which means at the mere age of twenty-eight, I am completely ruined for any other woman. And I don't even care. I want to revel in the ruin.

My brain on overload, I drive the rest of the way to the restaurant in silence, taking the curves at high speed, enjoying the way the tires stick to the road, the squeal of rubber on asphalt making me smile. I downshift, the whine of the engine like music to my ears, and the faster I drive, the more I get into it.

"You're crazy," she whispers as I gain speed, going close to one hundred on a straightaway a few miles from the restaurant.

I roll down the windows, let the cool night air wash over my heated skin. Her hair blows everywhere, even re- strained by the ponytail, and a long blonde strand hits me in the face, causing me to push it away. I chance a look at her, see that she's gripping the edge of her seat, her body on edge, her expression full of . . . excitement?

Really?

"You like it," I say, my tone practically a dare. "You're literally sitting on the edge of your seat."

"I do like it," she quietly admits, her wild eyes meeting mine. A shaky exhalation leaves her, and she nods toward me. "Go faster."

My foot presses on the gas pedal, picking up speed. She's watching me; I can feel her gaze on me, and I reach toward her, pushing all that sexy, wind-blown hair away from her face. Before I can drop my hand, she leans her cheek into my palm, then turns and presses a hot, wet kiss to my flesh, her tongue darting out for a quick lick.

I swear.

Ah, hell. I grow instantly hard, letting my hand fall from her cheek, but she wraps her fingers around my wrist, bringing my hand to her mouth and drawing my index finger deep inside her mouth, dragging her wet, lush lips along the length before she releases it, her eyes never leaving mine.

Easing my foot off the gas, I swallow hard. She's going to kill me. I tear my gaze from hers, keeping my attention on the road. It's dark, it feels like we're virtually alone, and I'm tempted. So tempted to pull over, kiss her until she's gasping my name, and then fuck her in the back seat just like I first envisioned.

I chance a glance at her, see the flushed cheeks, the parted lips. I recognize that look from last night. She's aroused.

Hell, yeah. So am I.

Downshifting, I pull over. I throw the car into park

and lean over the center console at the exact time she moves toward me. We attack each other, lips searching, hands wandering, clinging, fighting to draw our bodies closer, but the awkward space makes it difficult.

"I want you," she whispers against my mouth before she sucks my lower lip between hers. "Please."

"Seriously?" I'm in absolute shock. She acted like having sex with me was the biggest mistake of her life. But here she is leaning into my hands as I curve them around her breasts, her breaths coming out in sharp pants as she rests her hands over mine, making me squeeze her breasts together.

Damn, she's hot.

"Seriously." Her voice tinged with amusement, she withdraws from my touch, moving closer to the passenger side door. Slowly she reaches for the hem of her shirt and tugs it up, then off, tossing it onto the back seat. Her bra is black, smooth satin and my mouth waters as she reaches behind her, unclasping it and tearing it off so it falls from her fingertips onto the floorboard.

I can't form words. She strips off each article of clothing until she's completely naked, coming at me like a woman possessed. I feel like a man possessed, obsessed with the feel of her soft skin beneath my palms, the taste of her. She climbs on top of me, pressing all that hot, wet deliciousness against my denim-covered cock, grinding against me like she's trying to get off.

Shit. Maybe she is trying to get off.

But no. She wants to involve me in the action too. Her nimble fingers undo my button fly and she's reaching inside my boxer briefs, sure fingers curling around the length of my cock. Knowing I'm about to blow, I lightly slap her hand away, reaching behind me to pull out my wallet and the condom nestled within.

I packed extra in the glove compartment earlier. I'm not an idiot.

"You make me crazy," she whispers, snatching it out of my fingers. She tears into it, rolling the condom onto my cock and then she's on top of me, slowly sinking until I'm completely imbedded inside her.

A car drives by, the bright white lights flashing across her, offering me a glimpse of her swaying breasts, her hips as they slowly move up and down. I grasp her there, steadying her, keeping her slow, afraid I'll ruin it by coming too fast.

Because holy shit, I'm ready to explode. I'm still fully clothed save for my open jeans and she's deliciously naked. All that fragrant, soft skin is wrapped around me, her breasts in my face, nipples teasing my lips. I draw one in deep, sucking, tonguing, teasing her until she's tossing her head back, riding me relentlessly. I shift away from her, wanting to watch. She's beautiful in her abandon, so lost as she races toward that delicious moment, and I want to mark this moment permanently in my brain.

"So good," she breathes, tipping her head back down so she can press her forehead to mine. I tip my chin up, brush her mouth with mine and she devours me. The kiss hot, wet. Deep. I grip the end of her ponytail, tugging hard and she gasps.

Damn. She likes that too. If we didn't hate each other so much, I'd believe she was made just for me.

"Harder, Gage," she encourages, her hands gripping my shoulders. "Make me come."

Ah, fuck. I can't resist that. I increase my pace, thrusting hard, filling her again and again until she's crying out my name, her body quivering, sobs falling from her lips as she collapses against me.

I hold her close, tracing circles on her back with my fingertips, making her shiver. Her grip around my neck is like a vice, her face buried into my neck. I feel her warm lips press sweet kisses to my flesh, and I squeeze her closer, our racing hearts in complete and total sync.

"You haven't come yet," she whispers against my throat, her tongue licking.

My cock twitches. It's more than aware of that. "I know."

She lifts her head up, her arms loosely resting around my neck, her expression slumberous and full of satisfaction. "Let me make that up to you," she murmurs as she slowly starts to grind against me.

I wrap my hands around her waist, guiding her, my gaze locked where our bodies meet. She's moving on me slow and sure, little murmurs of pleasure escaping her, and I can't look away. I'm entranced by the way she moves, the words she says, the way she looks at me.

What am I doing? What is she doing to me? I feel lost . . . gloriously, deliciously lost in my need to have her.

Only her.

I'm closer to the edge, unable to hold back, when she reaches between us and touches my cock, then her clit. The sight of her slender fingers playing down there sends me right over the edge, making me gasp as my hips buck against her. She smiles her encouragement, murmuring my name, and I grab hold of her ponytail pulling her face to mine so I can drown in her kiss.

Fuck. I'm wrecked. All because of this woman.

Chapter Nine

─────────────────────

Marina

I ENTER THE building with my head held high, pretending I have everything completely under control, while inside I'm a confused mass of jumbled nerves and rapidly growing insecurities. Smoothing my hair back from my face, I glance toward Gage as he stops just beside me, tall and commanding, earning plenty of appreciative glances from the various women sitting in the lobby and waiting to be seated.

He finds me watching him and flashes me a dazzling smile, making my heart race. I remember what he looked like only minutes ago, dazed and fascinated with me as I rose above him, naked and greedy and crazed with wanting him. Riding his thick cock straight into oblivion.

I don't know what came over me. Watching him drive that powerful, outrageously expensive car, his big hand shifting the gears, his thighs flexing as he pressed the pedals, sent me into a sexual tizzy. Just like that, I wanted him. Had to have him at that very moment or felt like I was going to die. I've never reacted like that to a man.

Ever.

"Do I look okay?" I whisper, leaning into him as I tuck yet another tendril behind my ear. I'd slicked on fresh lipstick while still in the car, pulling my clothes into place as best I could. He'd barely done anything, just tucked himself back into his jeans, tugged on his sweater, and he was good to go.

Men. They're disgustingly easy sometimes.

"Truth?" He smiles, and I sort of want to punch him for being so ridiculously good looking. I feel like a frazzled mess while he looks amazing. His hair is a little messy—from my eager fingers, I might add—but it's a good look for him.

Everything's a good look for him.

"Of course, tell me the truth," I mutter, irritated. Great, I must look a complete mess if he feels the need to tell me the "truth." I wonder if I have time to dash into the bathroom and put myself back together before we have to go sit down with Archer and his fiancé.

I really hope I like his fiancé. I'm more nervous meeting her than talking with Archer. Women hold such a strong influence on their men and their decisions. I know Archer's a respected businessman, but from what I understand, he's so far gone over this new and very steady woman in his life, I'm sure he listens to her opinion.

So what if she hates me? She could tell Archer how she feels and *bam*. My chance is over.

Gage grabs hold of my elbow and tugs me closer to him, his mouth right at my ear, hot breath fanning against my skin and making me shiver before he whispers, "You look . . . freshly fucked. And beautiful with it."

I pull away to meet his gaze, utterly speechless.

He grins. "It's a good look on you. One I suggest you wear as often as possible."

I smile and follow through with my earlier instinct, giving him a slug on the arm. He smirks, leans in once more and kisses my cheek, his lips lingering, warm and soft and so comforting I want to melt. "I can keep you in that look all night if you want."

"Stop." I shove him away from me, noticing the strange looks we're receiving from those waiting for a table. Great.

I so don't want to draw attention to the two of us together. What if someone recognizes us and it gets back to my dad that I'm out on a date with Gage? From what Gage told me, he's tried to get in contact with my father numerous times since our first encounter. And I know he's tried to talk to him prior to our meeting too.

I'm basically hanging out with the enemy. My dad would be furious, though I haven't talked to him about Gage. I'm too scared. It's bad enough I told my mom his name. It didn't dawn on me at the time since I was too busy looking for something to wear and not thinking with all cylinders firing. I'd been a little brain-warped after our night together, and now? After the incident in the car?

I'm toast. Done.

"Considering I know just how much you enjoyed getting that particular look, I wanted to make the offer," he says from over his shoulder as he moves away from me, approaching the hostess's counter and asking if our other party has already been seated. He flicks his head for me to follow and I do so like a good little girlfriend, letting him take my hand, loving the way he entwines my fingers with his as he leads me through the restaurant.

I can't believe I've fallen into this role so easily. I shouldn't want to. I shouldn't do it at all. I'm not his girlfriend and he's not my boyfriend. We're not even in a real relationship.

We're at one of the most expensive and revered restaurants in Napa Valley. Gage and Archer have exquisite taste, I'll give them that. The place is overflowing with beautiful people, all of them dressed to perfection. I can't see anything but a sea of suits and finely cut dresses. They all look like they just came out of work.

I look like I'm ready to hang out for the night and go clubbin'. Or worse, I have the freshly fucked look, according to Gage. Can everyone see we just had wild and crazy sex in his car?

God, I hope not.

My fingers tremble, and I feel him squeeze my hand. He comes to a stop, turning to look at me, his face etched with concern. "You okay?"

I shouldn't let it touch me that he's being so sweet. But it does. I want to melt at the concern I see reflected in his eyes. "A little nervous," I admit.

"Archer won't bite. You're going to be fine." He kisses

me on the lips, right there in the middle of the freaking restaurant, and I want to both disappear and scream with glee that this man . . . this very fine man standing right here, is mine.

But he's not. Not really. We're . . . huh. I don't know what we're doing. He wants my family's property. He'd probably fall to my feet in gratitude if I introduced him to my father, which I so don't want to do. Helping him get that much closer to what he wants would be idiotic on my part. It would be the end of the bakery.

Besides, I want an opportunity to grow my business. Instead of pushing him away, I'm selfishly spending time with him. And we're gaining something from each other while we have wild passionate sex on the side. A totally unexpected bonus in this bargain we made.

It's so strange, so unlike anything I've ever done before. There is no definition for what I'm experiencing with Gage.

I just need to approach it day by day.

"What about Archer's fiancé?" I ignore the pointed stare the hostess is shooting us when she discovers we're not following behind her any longer. Just how big is this stupid restaurant?

"Yeah. Uh. She's great." He smiles and fidgets, releasing my hand so he can run his through his tousled dark hair. "I have a confession to make."

Dread fills my stomach. "What is it?"

"Sir? Miss? Your table is this way," the hostess calls, her voice full of hostility that we're not obeying her command.

We ignore her. "Tell me," I say when he still hasn't answered.

Shrugging, he reaches out, trails his index finger down my cheek. "She's my sister."

I frown. "Who? Do you mean Archer's fiancé?"

"Yeah." He winces. "My best friend is marrying my baby sister."

"Oh." I'm sort of offended that he didn't tell me from the first. Why keep it such a secret? I don't get it.

Sometimes, I really don't get him.

"Mister Emerson!" The hostess is practically shouting at us. "Please, follow me!"

We hurry after her, my mind awhirl after his confession. She leads us to the very back of the restaurant, where the private dining rooms are, and I blow out a slow, cleansing breath, trying to calm my agitated nerves.

I thought having sex with Gage in his car would take the edge off, but no, I couldn't have been more wrong. I feel edgier, more amped up than ever. He's not helping matters with how sweet he's being. You'd think I'd like his attitude and want more of it, after all the fighting and the arguing between us.

But I need the distance. I need to focus and think about what exactly I want to say to Archer. Now that I know he's with Gage's sister, that Archer is Gage's best friend, it puts a new spin on their relationship. Puts a new spin on the entire dynamic that's about to happen once we sit down with them. I knew he and Archer were good friends, but I guess I didn't realize they were *best* friends. They're practically family.

"Here you go." The hostess stops at an open door that leads to a small dining room, the interior done in cool greens and blues. Gage lets me walk in first, and I spot them sitting at the table. I smile nervously at Archer and his fiancé. Gage's freaking sister.

God help me, I hope I don't make a fool of myself in front of her. I want her to like me.

It doesn't matter if she likes you or not. You're not looking for a relationship with Gage. You're having dirty, awesome sex with him. Nothing more, nothing less.

I really wish I could believe that.

Plus, I need to focus on what I really want out of this dinner. A chance to gain exposure for the bakery and my aunt's desserts by having them featured at his hotel. That's what matters tonight.

Gage rests his hand at the small of my back, his simple touch making my heart hammer. I watch helplessly as Archer stands and approaches us, a warm smile on his handsome face as he stops in front of me. He's wearing a suit, just like everyone else in this restaurant save for me and Gage, and he's intimidating despite the friendly expression.

"Marina, it's wonderful to see you." Leaning in, he presses the requisite society kiss to my cheek. "You're looking ravishing tonight."

Oh. God. I want to die. He is so close to the truth it's embarrassing. Does he know Gage ravished me? Can he tell? Am I wearing a flashing sign on my forehead that screams *freshly fucked*?

Gage's low chuckle doesn't help matters either. If he

doesn't watch it, he's going to end up with an elbow in the ribs.

"Thank you," I say, my voice shaky, and I clear my throat. "So glad you're able to have dinner tonight with us, Archer. I know it was last minute."

"Anything for Gage." He flashes him a quick, smug smile. "I may think he's a complete asshole, but considering he's going to be my brother-in-law in less than a year, I guess I need to start thinking of him as part of my family."

"Oh, stop being so rude." His fiancé approaches us as well, her expression open. Friendly. Curious. "I'm Ivy. Gage's sister. You must be Marina." She extends her hand toward me.

"Nice to meet you," I offer weakly, overwhelmed as she takes my hand and shakes it. I don't want to screw this up, and I'm going to if I don't watch it. I can barely keep my crap together as I stand before these two people.

I need to chill out.

Ivy's wearing a red wrap-style dress, looking effortless and elegant, and again I feel like an idiot in my jeans. I blame working at the bakery for my lack of dressy clothes. I have them, I just don't bother wearing them much anymore. I'm always in jeans.

Though Gage doesn't seem to mind me in jeans . . .

We all sit at the table, Archer and Ivy resuming the spots they occupied and Gage and I sitting across from them. The table is small, the setting intimate, and I keep my gaze on the place setting in front of me, trying to calm my racing heart.

Gage settles his hand on my back, reaching up to tickle at the sensitive skin of my nape. I jerk my gaze toward him, giving him a look I hope he can interpret: one that says *stop touching me*.

He doesn't seem to get it. Clueless bastard. Instead he's smiling at me, as if he enjoys my slight discomfort, and I grimace at him, my breath catching in my throat when he laughs at me.

"Why are you so worked up?" he asks after the waiter sweeps out of the room with our drink orders. "You seem upset."

"I'm not upset." I glance toward Archer and Ivy, who are arguing over what to order for dinner. God, they're cute. "I feel woefully underdressed compared to everyone else in this stupid restaurant."

His smile turns wicked as he leans in closer, his voice lowering. "Baby, when we were in my car just a few minutes ago? Now *that* was woefully underdressed."

His words set my cheeks on fire, and he chuckles, shaking his head. "One minute you're the sexiest, most naked thing I've ever seen, and now you're blushing like a sweet schoolgirl."

"There's no such thing as 'most naked,' Gage," I say irritably, earning a bigger grin for my effort. "You're either naked or you're not."

"Well. You were *very* naked." He kisses my cheek. Again. It's like he can't stop touching me, not that I'm protesting. "And right now? You look amazing."

I feel my cheeks heat further, which is silly. Three simple words and my heart is hammering. He touches my elbow, my back, tucks my hair behind my ear, and I want him to touch me more. I think he sees it too. His knowing smile—which I should find completely annoying—instead sends a shivery little thrill down my spine.

"You don't think I should be wearing a dress?" Why am I acting like a simpering, self-conscious girlfriend? I need to stop.

His gaze roves over me, taking me all in, and my skin heats as if he's physically touched me. "I think you look perfect," he says when his eyes finally meet mine, dark and serious and so intense I can hardly look away.

Oh. My. What is happening between us? I don't ... don't know what comes over me when I'm with him. He's acting like he's truly interested in me and I . . . just don't think that's possible. Sexually, we're compatible. But two people can be in a sexual relationship that doesn't go beyond that point, right? Not that I've ever experienced anything like that, but I know people do it all the time.

So why is he looking at me like that? Saying such deliciously wonderful things to me? What in the world are we doing? This is supposed to be temporary between us.

Yet it already feels all too real. It shouldn't though. Not at all.

Someone clears their throat, and I tear my gaze away from Gage to find Archer studying us, his expression full of amusement. Ivy's studying us as well, her delicate brow furrowed in confusion.

I can't blame her. I'm confused too.

"So Marina, I hear you've been spending time with Gage," Archer says, one brow lifting.

I want to squirm in my seat. Are Gage and I that obvious? Of course we are. We're hanging all over each other like we're together. He can't keep his hands off me. We just had sex in his car on the side of the road, for the love of God. The pheromones or whatever between us are probably off the charts.

And if they're best friends like Gage said, then surely Archer must know all about Gage's romantic past. Maybe I'm not Gage's normal type, and he's confused as well?

"Have you met Ivy before?" Archer asks me before he studies his fiancé with unabashed love in his eyes.

He knows the answer to this question. Is Archer trying to make this evening more awkward? What should I say?

Oh hey, Ivy. I know we haven't met and all but I've known your brother for a few days and we're having the wildest sex of my life. How do you do?

"This is the first time. I've only known Gage for a short time so . . ." I smile at her and she smiles warmly in return. "I had no idea Gage had a sister, so it's wonderful to meet you."

"I had no idea Gage was seeing someone, so the feeling's mutual." Her smile fades as her gaze turns assessing. "I don't believe I've heard my brother mention you before. How did you two meet exactly?"

"Um . . ." My voice trails off and I feel silly. I sought him out that night. *I wanted to meet the man who's trying to buy out my family.*

But I can't tell Ivy that. I'd sound like a cold, callous bitch.

"I'm so curious. Gage never lets me meet any of the

women that he dates." Ivy's just about as determined as her brother. Scary.

And have there been a lot of women? There had to have been. He's charming, sexy, rich, and influential. What woman wouldn't find him a catch?

You, maybe?

"At that wine- and beer-tasting event I went to in Archer's place," Gage answers for me.

"That was only a few nights ago," Ivy says, frowning.

Gage shrugs. "Right. That's what I said. We met, and I asked her out. Now here we are." He sends Archer a pointed look, who just smirks at him in return, and I don't know what to think.

There's an undercurrent flowing between these three, unspoken messages, and I'm the one left out. I knew this would happen. I have no idea what's going on, and I don't like it. I wish we could go back to the car, where it's just the two of us. Wrapped up in our own little bubble, touching each other, kissing each other . . .

Getting lost in one another.

Chapter Ten

Gage

"I DON'T KNOW if I want to go to your bakery," Ivy says with a laugh, making me glare at her. She waves her hand, dismissing me easily, considering she's been doing it since we were kids.

But damn, I don't want her to offend Marina. She's sensitive enough about her family business.

They're laughing though. Having a good time together. Archer leans back in his chair with an arrogant expression on his face. Like he has me all figured out and knows that I'm already halfway whipped when it comes to this woman.

Not that I'd ever admit he's right.

"Trust me, I feel the same way sometimes! God, the things my aunt can create. Her breakfast muffins are to die for. If I didn't watch myself so carefully, I'd end up fat as can be." Marina laughs, the sound warming me deep inside, and I chance a look at her.

She's beautiful. Her eyes are sparkling and her smile is wide. My sister looks happy. This was exactly what I wanted to avoid and look at the two of them. Hitting it off and acting like they're old friends.

What a night it's been. We've actually been getting along, making conversation that didn't involve us calling each other names or me saying something infinitely stupid.

I had one minor slipup. Well, a few, if I count the most recent blunder me confessing that Ivy is my sister. I think that sort of blew Marina's mind.

We're getting along now. Everything's rockin'. I still can't believe the way she attacked me in my car. Talk about the hottest experience of my life. I've never done something that wild, never had a woman jump me after becoming aroused by my driving my freaking car.

I barely know her, and yet I feel like this woman sitting at my side was made for me.

Marina's had a couple of glasses of wine, and the alcohol has loosened her up. Maybe the sex earlier did too, I don't know. She's pretty damn easygoing, and I like it.

I like her.

The scent of her hair drives me crazy. It wafts toward me every time she turns her head, her ponytail swinging. I love the sound of her laughter. I haven't heard it very often, but I plan on changing that. I love her smile too. She's very expressive, all that cool blonde mystery from the first night I met her seemingly evaporated. In its place is an open, smiling woman. Full of laughter and easy conversation, sexy as hell wearing that thin, glittery black top that dips low in the front, offering me a generous view of her cleavage.

Breasts I had my hands all over not an hour ago. Her nipples were in my mouth. I can still hear her ragged moans when I sucked them deep. I remember her naked body, wrapped all around me as she rode me hard.

Yeah. Fuck. This woman . . . she's blowing my mind.

Ivy had been wary at first. I don't normally bring women around her, and we threw her for a loop when she found out we'd only just met. She knows I haven't been serious about a woman in a long time. If ever.

"We should definitely do that," Marina says with an enthusiastic nod.

Her words bring me back down to earth. "Do what?" I ask her, glancing from my sister back to Marina.

She turns to look at me, those sparkling blue eyes trained on my face, making my blood burn. For her. "Oh, your sister suggested we go on a shopping trip together soon. I was just telling her how it's been forever since I went clothes shopping, and she offered to go with me into San Francisco for the day. Sounds like fun, don't you think?"

Reality butts its ugly head into my mind, and I frown. The two of them are almost getting too close when this . . . thing between Marina and I will go nowhere. Because that's what always happens. Yeah, I'm into this woman more than I've been with any woman, but I know my patterns. This won't last. It never does. "You're not constantly shopping, huh? I thought that's what all women do."

"Oh my God," Ivy mutters while Archer full-out groans.

Marina glares at me, her eyes narrow, her lips tight. "I cannot believe you just said that. Are you for real?"

There I go again, saying the worst thing ever and offending Marina. Thought I had it under control since we've been getting along so well tonight, but I guess not. I swear it's like my brain shuts down when I'm around her, and I blurt out the stupidest things with absolutely no thought. "I was kidding?" I offer weakly.

"Yeah right," she mumbles, her eyes hot with anger as they shoot daggers at me.

If looks could kill . . .

Hell, I can't tell if she's really mad or not.

Archer stands. "Hey Gage, come with me for a minute. I want to show you something."

"What do you want to show me?" Now I'm confused. Maybe I'm the one who's had too much wine. Or maybe I'm just drunk on Marina . . .

"Let's go outside," he says with a giant smile on his face, but it looks fake as hell.

I follow him outside wordlessly, the front of the restaurant still crowded with people waiting for a table. We end up around the side of the building, the cool night air washing over me as a breeze blows over us, relieving my overheated body and brain.

"What the hell is going on in there?" Archer asks.

Shrugging, I glance around, making sure no one is paying attention to us. "What are you talking about?"

"I'm confused. You seem way into Marina, and I thought you weren't interested in her. Marina and Ivy seem to like each other. Which is great, I'm glad to see the two of them getting along so well so quick, but I thought . . . I thought this dinner was all about Marina wanting to talk to me about some proposition she has," Archer says, running a hand through his hair.

"I think she's nervous. That's why she hasn't mentioned anything to you yet," I suggest. Hell, I'd told her not to say anything, and here's Archer asking why she's not. I'm just making up excuses, and it's not like we can call her out on it at the table. That would just be flat-out rude.

Since when do you care if you're rude to Marina or not?

It irritates that she hasn't even told me what she wants to talk to Archer about. I'm just as much in the dark as he is. Doesn't she trust me enough with the information?

Of course not, asshole. Remember? She doesn't even know you.

"Well. She's hardly said one word to me, but that's fine. Maybe she doesn't want to talk about it in front of your sister, which I totally get." Archer pauses, studying me. "And then there's you."

"What about me?" I'm immediately defensive.

"If this is, and I quote, 'a business proposition,' and you're just using her, and I quote again, 'to get what you want,' then you're doing a damn good job of being the attentive, googly-eyed date."

"'Googly-eyed?' Nice description," I mutter. We're obvious. I didn't think it would matter in front of Archer and Ivy, but what the hell was I thinking? It didn't help that we just had sex before we stumbled into the restaurant. I still had a postcoital glow going on, for fuck's sake.

"It's true! Every time you look at her, you're like a love-sick puppy. I think you like her," Archer says.

"I do not," I answer way too quickly. Misery courses through me. Do I like her? I shouldn't like her.

You fucking like her, moron.

"I'm attracted to her," I finally say. "How could I not be? She's beautiful."

Archer shakes his head. "Then you better be up-front with her about this real estate deal you want to make with her dad."

"No way. She'll hate me for it." She called me a scum-sucking shark or whatever the first time we met, when she discovered who I am. She finds out I want to sweep in on the property the Molinas hold on St. Helena's Main Street—including the very bakery she's running—she'll hate me for life.

Shit. She probably already suspects this. She has to. Marina's no dummy. She's smart and beautiful and—

"She'll hate you more if you keep the truth from her."

I absorb Archer's words, remaining quiet. Since when did he get so good at doling out advice? That's always been my thing. Now I'm the one making idiot moves, and he's the stable, secure one full of logic.

"You could always lease the property back to her," he suggests when I don't say anything. "Give her a deal and let her run the bakery that seems to mean so much to her."

"How do you know what it means to her?" I ask incredulously.

"Weren't you listening to what she said? She was talking about running the bakery, her aunt, and the amazing cakes she makes. I've tasted them, so has Ivy. She was totally engrossed in the conversation, offering Marina all sorts of marketing ideas to try." Archer shakes his head. "Are you oblivious or what?"

I look at Marina and all I can think about is the next time I can get her naked. I guess . . . I was tuning her out like a self-absorbed asshole.

"I'm going back in there and asking her what she wants to talk about. I'm not in the mood for a bunch of pussyfooting anymore. I'm too damn curious," Archer finally says, starting to head back to the front of the building.

I walk with him, the both of us striding side by side toward the restaurant entrance. "Come on. Let her segue into it on her own. I think she just needs to build up her courage."

"She's having fun with Ivy, and she's probably had a little bit too much to drink. I think it's time for Marina to grow a pair and tell me what's up." Archer throws open the door, and I follow him in, wondering at his change of mood.

He's never been the most patient person. While I have no problem lying in wait, calculating my every move. Whether in business or personal matters, Archer gets too antsy.

"Give her time, damn it," I mutter, earning a hard glare from Archer.

"Why are you so protective of her, huh? You've only known her a few days. What gives?"

I care for her. It's the stupidest thing ever, but I do. I

like her. A lot. The more I think about Archer's leasing suggestion, the more I believe it could be the solution to the problem hovering over us. "I—"

"You like her," Archer says again, not sounding surprised. "A lot. I get it, man. Sometimes when it happens, it takes a while like it did for Ivy and me. Other times, it happens so fast you just know."

"I just know what?"

"You know you're in love with her."

I scoff. "I am not in love with her," I say emphatically. "I've known her a week."

"You have feelings for her, then." Archer grimaces. "Christ, listen to me. I've turned into Oprah."

"I blame Ivy," I say with a grin, though deep inside my stomach is knotted, my head spinning. Fine. I like Marina. A lot. I'm not in love with her. Not . . .

Yet?

I banish the thought.

"Be honest with her." Archer stabs his finger into my chest, making me wince. "If I can give you any advice, it's to tell her the truth. Be up-front. Let her know about the real estate deal. Tell her you want her help in getting to talk to her father."

"I sort of already did," I say, rubbing at my chest where he poked me. Damn, that hurt.

He's right though. I don't have to take the bakery away from her. I don't want to. If it means that much to her, I'm sure we could work something out. I could lease the building back to her and her aunt and they could keep Autumn Harvest open. Keep the business in the family.

That's a freaking great idea.

"Great. Good. You're on the right path." Archer exhales loudly. "It's just . . . I like seeing the two of you together. Don't make fun of my ass, but you seem really happy with her. You're always so wrapped up in your work. It's nice to see you let loose and have fun."

I run my hand across the back of my neck, contemplating his words. "You're not saying this because of that stupid bet we made, are you?"

He rolls his eyes. "I already lost that fucker and you know it. Why would I want to sabotage your ass? I have no stake in it. This is between you and Matt."

"I haven't seen him in—forever." Matt's busy getting his new winery ready for its grand opening.

"Ivy's with him a lot lately since she's been working on the interiors. Ask her how he's doing." Archer smiles.

We head back to the private dining room. "What's up with the shit-eating grin?"

Archer shrugs. "Ivy thinks Matt's assistant has a major crush on him. He ignores her. I think it makes her want him more."

"Who the hell would have a crush on Matt DeLuca?" I ask indignantly. Only the majority of the female population in California, let alone the entire United States. Back in the day, he'd been the star pitcher for the San Francisco Giants. Until a major knee injury put him into early retirement. Thank Christ for lucrative investments and endorsements. The guy sits on pile of gold bricks, he's so damn rich.

Huh. There's another reason why I'm not looking for a

serious relationship. I don't want Matt to win this stupid bet. But is that good enough reason to not want to pursue something more with Marina? So I can beat Matt in a million-dollar bet?

Shit. Am I really considering if Marina is worth more than a million dollars?

You are . . .

Archer's out of the running with our bet. I'm close to being out without even realizing it. So that leaves Matt the winner?

Unless he finds himself attached as well in the next few weeks, months. Whatever. Then we'd have to call it a draw.

"You should have Ivy do some matchmaking," I suggest casually, knowing Archer will see right through me.

"Good idea." Archer nods as we stop at the open door of our dining room. "I'll talk to Ivy. She can work some magic and hook them up."

"And then I'm off the hook," I finish, making Archer grin.

We enter the private dining room chuckling, Ivy and Marina silent as we resume our seats. "You two okay?" Ivy asks pointedly.

I slip my arm around the back of Marina's chair, stroking her shoulder with the tips of my fingers. "We're great. How are you two?"

Marina turns to look at me, her expression full of confusion. "I thought you were arguing or something."

"I was just trying to set his ass straight," Archer pipes up. I send him a hard stare. Wish he would shut the fuck up.

"So Marina, why don't we discuss whatever it is you wanted to talk about with me?"

She fidgets in her chair, glancing down for a moment and breathing deep, as if for courage before she lifts her head, her gaze meeting Archer's. "You want to talk about it now?"

"Now is as good a time as any," he says with a shrug.

"Okay." She rests her hands on the table, her fingers plucking nervously at the pale blue tablecloth. "Like I was saying earlier, my aunt Gina makes amazing cakes."

"They are amazing," Archer agrees. "I can personally vouch for that."

She smiles. "Thank you. I'll let her know. Well, I wanted to see if you were interested in featuring her cakes at the restaurants within your hotels."

Archer studies her, doesn't say a word. He's thinking, I can practically see the wheels turning in his brain, but his silence is making Marina uncomfortable. "I like this idea," he finally says with a small nod.

"You do?" Marina sounds so hopeful I can practically feel the excitement vibrating off her.

"I do. We can call the cakes 'decadent desserts' or something along those lines. Our resorts have an almost ... hedonistic quality to them." Archer smiles. "You and Gage should stay there sometime."

Very funny, motherfucker.

"Gina is a creative genius. Not only do her desserts and muffins taste amazing, but they're beautiful. Like little pieces of edible art."

"Hmm." Archer taps his finger against his pursed

lips, then reaches inside his pocket and pulls out his cell phone, bringing up his calendar. "Can you meet with me on Monday? Come up with a written proposal, exactly what you want to provide, and I'll consult with my restaurant managers, see if they're on board."

Marina's mouth is hanging open. She looks totally shocked. "Are you serious?" she asks breathlessly.

"Absolutely. I was just telling Ivy how I wanted to stop by your bakery soon so I could get a cake. I have a not-so-secret sweet tooth and so does Ivy. Occasionally we indulge. And your aunt is amazing." Archer smiles. "I'd be honored if I could feature her at the restaurant. There will be some kinks to work out, but I know we can make it happen if you're both patient."

Marina pushes out of her chair and goes to Archer, throwing her arms around him and hugging him so tight, I'm afraid her cleavage is going to strangle him. I refuse to get jealous. She's so happy I can't begrudge her or her happiness. Ivy's laughter indicates she feels the same way.

"Thank you, thank you," Marina says, jumping away from him, the smile on her face saying it all. "We'll make this happen. I promise. You won't regret it."

"I know I won't," Archer says, smiling at her in return before he levels his gaze on me. "Hope everything works out for you and the bakery. If anything, your aunt could come and work for me if Autumn Harvest ends up getting shut down."

That fucking prick. I can't believe he would say that to her.

"Um, I'm hoping we can make it work, but I appreciate you offering a job to Gina. I know she would appreciate it too." Marina smiles, though some of the light has dimmed. "Thanks, Archer." The excitement has left her voice. She sounds disappointed and she glances down at the table.

Damn my friend for putting her on top of the world and then knocking her right off with a few choice words.

"Why would you say that to her?" Ivy slaps his arm, hard. "You give her good news only to bring her crashing down with bad stuff."

"Hey, I'd hire Marina too." Archer flashes her a smile, which Marina returns, but it doesn't quite light up her eyes.

Jerk. Thank God my sister spoke up. He's as bad as me, saying the wrong thing at the wrong time.

Hearing his offer makes me want to help her keep the bakery now more than ever. If I get my hands on those buildings, there is no doubt in my mind I will make that bakery hers. She can fight me all she wants, but I won't take no for an answer.

I want to do right by her. It's the least I can do.

Chapter Eleven

Gage

"I'm nervous." I tap my fingers against the steering wheel, nodding my head to the music playing on the radio.

Marina reaches over and grabs my hand, squeezing quickly before she releases it. "Don't be. He's going to love you. Maybe."

Ha. How honest of her. The "he" she's referring to is her father. The man I've been trying to see for months so I can make an offer hopefully he can't refuse. Scott Knight has avoided me. Yeah, I know he's been out of town a lot, but the least he could do is take my calls.

Now he has no choice. I'm going to dinner tonight with Marina at her house and meeting the parents. A big step for me, one I rarely make, but we've been seeing each other for over a month. Hopefully, Scott and I can discuss the real estate deal further. Maybe.

Funny how once I got involved with his daughter, that deal isn't as important to me anymore.

"I'm pretty sure your dad hates me," I say, because it's true. The guy must despise me. He's avoided me because he doesn't want to make the deal. Now he probably hates the fact I'm with his daughter. His only child. God, I'd hate me if I were him.

Could I sound any more ridiculous? I'm anxious as fuck and acting like an idiot.

She doesn't say a word in response to my dumb statement. Just sits in the passenger seat of my car with that blissed-out expression on her face. The one that says *I just got laid,* which she did since we had sex right before we left.

I frown. Hope her parents won't know that look. They might want to kill me for touching their baby girl.

"Stop frowning." She leans over the center console and gives me a soft kiss on the lips—while I'm driving. Thank God the road is pretty empty because I swerve a little when that sweet mouth brushes against mine. "You worry too much."

Ha. I don't worry enough. I've been letting myself forget everything and just enjoying my time with Marina. If we're not working, we're together. And lately, I'm not working much at all, which means . . .

"Turn here," she instructs as she points her finger, breaking my train of thought, and I hit the brakes to slow down, turning right onto a long, tree-lined driveway. It seems to go on for miles and my stomach cramps with nerves at the thought of coming face-to-face with Scott

Knight. I haven't met a woman's family as her boyfriend since I don't know when. Ever?

This fact should make me feel like a twenty-eight-year-old loser, but damn it, I haven't found the right woman yet. As crazy as it sounds, in the little time we've known each other, I'm starting to think she's it. She's the one. Marina.

Shit. I know my friends love this. Archer doesn't fault me too hard because he's hopelessly in love with my sister. Matt, on the other hand, revels in my lovesick misery. He's also figuratively holding his hand out every chance he gets, demanding we hand over that one-million-dollar payout.

Jackass.

"How long is this damn driveway?" I mutter, earning a little laugh from Marina. Just as I ask, the thick trees disappear, revealing a circular driveway and a somewhat modest house with a spectacularly landscaped yard. I figured for sure Marina grew up in a sprawling mansion, the lone child who ran the house.

Guess I was wrong.

I park the Maserati in front of the four-car garage—the one sign of excess I see—surprised when Marina leans over and gives me another kiss. This one is longer, her lips lingering on mine, her hand curling around the back of my neck and holding me close. I exhale on a rough sound of pleasure and part her lips with my tongue, letting myself sink into her delicious, seductive mouth for a while. Forgetting all about my worry and the fact that I'm making out with Marina in front of her parents' home.

You're fucking making out with Marina in front of her parents' house, you asshole! What the hell? Are you sixteen and can't control yourself?

Well. That was like an ice-cold dose of reality.

Pulling out of the kiss, I smudge my thumb across her lush bottom lip, smiling at her as she glares up at me. I don't think she likes that I ended our kissing session. "We shouldn't be doing this," I whisper.

She pouts. "Why? I can't resist you. You know this."

Her simple admission makes me smile, but I don't let myself get too hung up on it. "We're at your house. Your parents are waiting inside to meet me, and I want to make the right impression. Not be the guy who's caught kissing and feeling up their daughter in his car."

"You weren't feeling me up," she points out.

I grin. "Yet."

Marina rolls her eyes. "Whatever. And don't worry about my dad. He'll take one look at your precious car and fall in love." Smiling, she leans in for another kiss, but I dodge her at the last minute, making her pout again. "Come on."

"Yeah, you got that right. Come on." I open the door and climb out, rounding the front so I can open her door. "Let's go meet your parents."

I take her hand and pull her out of the car, hoping like hell she doesn't notice my sweaty palm. She flashes me a sweet smile and leads me to the front door, her hips swishing seductively when she walks, her ass looking perfect in those jeans she's wearing.

Yeah. I'm a total goner for her. And she knows it too. I

never, ever thought a woman would have me so totally by the balls, but this one does. I don't mind either. In fact, I like it, knowing she's mine. Knowing I'm hers.

Archer finds my capitulation into couplehood amusing. My sister thinks it's the cutest thing she's ever seen, and that's a direct quote. Matt laughs every time I talk to him, asking if I'm completely whipped yet. He knows how reluctant I was to let myself get caught by a woman.

Now I'm walking into the so-called trap and seriously thinking I never want out of it.

Marina doesn't bother ringing the doorbell, and we walk inside to find the living area empty. It's a wide, open space, full of comfortable furniture that has seen better days and lots of family photos on every available flat surface. On tables, bookshelves, hung on the walls, I'm surrounded by Molinas and Knights, all of them watching me, making me want to squirm where I stand.

Yeah. I think I've lost my damn mind. This is what a case of nerves does to a man.

"Dad!"

Marina lets go of my hand, and I watch as she hurries toward her father who's just entered the living room. She practically throws herself at him, giving him a big hug, which he returns. I know they're close. She complains that she hasn't seen him much lately since he's been out of town, working all the time.

He's scrambling. Trying to sell off property and cars and whatever else he can get rid of to gain some cash flow. I know this through friends and acquaintances in the business. They all talk. Knight's been going into San

Francisco a lot lately to broker deals. Yet he's still holding on to that one property I want.

And I think if I work it just right, I can make it mine.

You are such a complete asshole. Marina's going to think you're using her to get to her dad.

That had been true, once upon a time. Not any longer. I care for this woman. Hell, I'm falling in love with her. Being in the middle of this situation, not quite knowing what to do . . .

It sucks.

"Good to see you, sweetheart." Her father gives Marina a kiss on the cheek, smiling down at her. "You look happy."

I stand there, at a loss over what I should do. Approach them? Clear my throat? Yell that his daughter looks happy because I put that smile on her face and the glow in her cheeks?

Yeah. Can't do that.

"I want you to meet Gage. Remember I told you about him?" She withdraws from her father's embrace and leads him over to where I stand. "Gage, this is my father, Scott."

"Nice to meet you." I offer my hand and he takes it, somewhat reluctantly. Or maybe I'm overreacting. The guy sets me on edge just looking at him.

He's tall, has a headful of salt-and-pepper hair, and his eyes are a pale, icy blue. Looking at me like he wants to hang me up by my balls too. "Gage. I believe you've been trying to get in contact with me."

"Let's not talk business today," Marina starts, but I interrupt her.

"I have been. I know you're a busy man, but when you get a chance, there's something I'd like to discuss with you."

"Call my office. We can set up a meeting," he offers breezily.

"I've been trying to do that for months," I tell him, needing him to know I'm not in the mood to play games.

Marina shoots me a horrified glare. "Gage," she whispers, trying to shut me up.

"Don't get mad at him. He's right." Scott's smile is easy. Too easy. "I have avoided his calls. I believe he's asking for something I'm not quite ready to give up yet."

Marina's mouth drops open. "How do you—"

"Just like you know," Scott says, smiling at her. "Everyone knows. This town is big, but it has a small-town feel, just like the gossip. And when a stranger comes into town, eager to buy up all the prime real estate he can, he gives everyone something to talk about."

I can't tell if this guy is merely tolerating me or hates my guts or . . . doesn't mind that I'm here and dating his daughter. His only child who I know he's very protective of.

Can't blame him though. I'm feeling rather protective of her too. Something we definitely have in common.

"Ah, is this your young man?" Maribella Knight breezes into the room, a slight smile curling her lips. This is who Marina gets her looks from. Maribella is a beautiful woman, her features so similar to her daughter's, I pretty much know what Marina's going to look like when she's older.

"Yes. This is Gage." Marina smiles nervously. Just like her relationship with her father is so strong, the one she shares with her mother is a bit more fragile. "Gage, this is my mom, Maribella."

"Call me Mari." She extends her hand toward me, her gaze not as warm as her voice.

I take her hand and give it a shake, notice how limp it is in my grip. "A pleasure," I say truthfully.

"I'm sure." The smile she offers me is brittle, and her gaze narrows the slightest bit.

Yeah. I don't think Marina's mother likes me very much at all.

Marina

I KNEW MY mother wouldn't like very Gage much. I don't think she'd like any man I brought home. She has these certain expectations I'm afraid no guy could ever meet.

So I pretended her cold disdain doesn't bother me. Throughout the afternoon and into dinner, she acted disinterested in him. But he did seem to get along with Dad. Now that shocks me. I figured my father would hate him on sight, considering Gage wants nothing more than to buy as much property from him as possible.

They have things in common though. They're both savvy businessmen. My father's only downfall is that he owned too much, too fast. It's been hard for him to recover from the economic crash.

And they both love cars. In fact, their conversation revolved mostly around cars from the time we arrived.

Gage even took Dad outside to check out his Maserati, which was love at first sight. At first I thought it was cute. After a while, I got bored.

Last, I'm hoping that they both care about me. Well, I know my dad loves me because, hello, he's my father. But Gage? He's never said the words to me, not that I think he would. He's never even admitted that he cares about me, but what can I expect? We haven't been together that long.

But Mom said something to me years ago, and I've never forgotten her words.

Sometimes, when you know, you just know.

That's how I feel about Gage. It scares the crap out of me and makes me want to punch him—because near violence is my usual mode of operation when it comes to Gage—but really, I'm excited. Nervous.

I'm falling in love.

Finally, I was able to drag him and my father apart, and we left long after dinner. Mom gave me a look that said she expected me to come right back. Dad told Gage to come by the office any time, or at the very least, call.

So strange. I thought my father would hate him. I thought I would hate Gage, but look at me. Maybe it's not such a bad thing, letting the bakery go. Gage could buy the strip of buildings, and my family would be in a better financial position. I know that's been my father's goal for a while. Maybe I'm the selfish one, wanting to hold on to a business that's nothing but a drain for my family.

"You're awfully quiet."

I glance up to find Gage flashing me a quick smile

before he returns his attention to the road. It's near ten o'clock and he has the windows cracked, letting in the cool fall air. The roads are virtually abandoned, the night sky is like dark velvet dotted with brightly twinkling stars shining from above, and I haven't felt this content in a long time. If ever.

"I'm glad you and my father got along so well," I say.

"Truthfully? I'm surprised," he admits.

Laughing, I shake my head. "So am I. I thought he might hate you . . . or love you."

"I know." Gage chuckles. "He's a good guy though. I like him."

"So are you. A good guy," I say softly, drinking Gage in, arousal heating my blood. It doesn't take much for me to want him. And seeing him behind the wheel of one of his powerful cars always makes me want to jump his bones.

When it comes to Gage, I'm incredibly weak. But I don't mind, because when I'm with him, I feel strong. Like I can do anything.

"Archer called yesterday." He sends me a quick look. "He said the two of you met a few days ago."

"We did." I nod. "He wanted to hammer out the details."

"That's amazing. I'm happy for you. Why didn't you tell me about it?" He sounds a little incredulous.

Leave it to Gage to get right to the point. Not that I can blame him. He deserves to know what's going on. "I was afraid I'd jinx it."

"Even to me?" He looks wounded. Silly man.

Leaning over the console, I press a kiss to his cheek, resting my hand on his muscular thigh so I can give it a squeeze. "Especially to you. You'll pump me up and get me so excited, I'll believe I can do no wrong. What if it didn't work out?"

"I would never let it not work out." His expression goes tight and his lips thin. "I'd kick Archer's ass before that would happen."

"That's exactly why I didn't tell you," I say, laughing. "This is not about you kicking Archer's ass. This is about Archer and me coming to a business decision. I can't have you glowering in the background, out to tear anyone apart who dares defy me."

"Why not? I can't help it if I'm protective of you."

He is so sweet I almost want to cry. Or do him. I'd prefer the latter.

"I love how protective you are of me," I murmur, smoothing my hand up and down his thigh. God, I love his body. He's so hard . . . everywhere. "I've never had someone defend me before."

"Well, I'm all yours. Don't forget it." He flinches and yelps when I cup his burgeoning erection. "Damn it, Marina. I'm driving."

"Yes, you are. And I'm touching you. Don't mind me." I undo the button fly on his jeans and slip my hand within, encountering warm, thin cotton stretched across his hard, thick cock. My panties dampen just touching him, and I release a shuddering breath.

"Don't you dare do what I think you're doing," he admonishes but his voice is weak. He's such a sucker for my touch.

Almost as much as I'm a sucker for his.

"I could give you a hand job while you drive." I scooch closer to him, my mouth at his ear, and I curl my fingers around his length. "Or a blow job. Remember when I did that last week?"

That had been fun. He'd been driving this powerful car, looking so sexy and in command I hadn't been able to resist. Next thing I knew, I was sprawled across the front seat of the Maserati with my head in his lap and his erection in my mouth. He'd had to pull over so I could finish him off without him wrecking.

Hot. He makes me so hot it's ridiculous. I'm with him, and I feel like a giddy teenager just out for a good time. I think he feels the same way.

At least we're in this together.

"Baby, I love it when you put your mouth on me, but I'm trying to get us home in one piece so I can have my mouth all over *you*." He stifles a groan when I deliberately stroke him. "Fuck, I swear you like seeing me in agony."

I do. I love torturing him. Only because I know he wants me so bad. It's a heady feeling, wielding this much power over Gage. And he has power over me as well, there's no denying it. I think we make a great team.

I can only hope my family feels the same. And eventually they can forgive him—specifically my mother—when he buys up our properties in downtown St. Helena and resells it. That's what his plan is. He doesn't even have to tell me. I already know.

And I finally think I'm okay with his plan. If I have to give up the bakery, then so be it. It chokes me up to think about it, but I need to act like a grownup. Archer and I have discussed my possibly working with him very casually, and I know he means his offer. He's mentioned me taking on a management position within one of his restaurants. I don't know if I would actually pursue it, but hey, it's an option. One I appreciate Archer making for me.

"We'll be home soon, okay?" He settles his hand over mine, giving it a squeeze. I, in turn, give his cock another squeeze. His ragged moan sends a little thrill through me that urges me to keep going. "And then you can do whatever you want to me."

"Really? Whatever I want?" I raise my brows. There are so many things we haven't attempted yet that I'd love to try out. I'm so comfortable with him, I know whatever I suggest, he'd be game for it.

"Definitely whatever you want. But you need to get your hand off my dick. I feel like I'm gonna blow," he says through gritted teeth.

I burst out laughing. "I've barely touched you!"

"Yeah, but that's all it takes, Marina. Haven't you realized that by now?" He turns to look at me, the heated glow in his eyes so intense, it steals my breath.

And makes my heart expand. He's so far gone over me, I love it.

Especially since I feel the same exact way.

Chapter Twelve

Gage

I'VE WAITED FOR this moment for what feels like a lifetime. Hounded this man until I'm sure he was sick and tired of hearing and seeing my name. Now that the time has come, and I'm sitting across from him in my San Francisco office, and despite being on my turf I'm so full of nerves I swear I'm going to be sick.

I am also a complete wuss. My biggest fear? That I'll somehow fuck it all up and lose everything.

Including Marina.

"My daughter likes you," Scott Knight says, his gaze razor sharp as it meets mine. I don't back down. Just keep my expression neutral and hope like hell he can't tell I'm sweating beneath my suit. "But just because she likes you doesn't mean I have to."

Jesus. Way to boost my confidence.

"I'm giving you the benefit of the doubt though.

Marina doesn't make bad choices. She's a smart girl. I like to think I had something to do with that." Scott turns his head toward the window, seemingly lost in thought. "So with that said, I think it's time we discuss you purchasing the property downtown."

Fucking finally. I practically sag in my chair. The relief that's ready to consume me is strong, but I'd also have to be an idiot to believe all is well. This could be a trick.

I've been tricked before.

But no. Without hesitation, he launches into the specifics. Costs and current leases and documents and the details regarding the preliminary contract he had his lawyer draw up. Photos and the history of the buildings and that one single question: *I don't plan on tearing it all down so I can rebuild, do I?*

Hell no, I answer, knowing that I pleased him just by the look on his face.

I scan all the documents as he pushes them toward me, knowing I'm going to have my lawyer review them anyway, so I don't read them over too carefully beyond the asking price. Nod my head in all the right places and ask the appropriate questions when prompted. But all the while I'm wondering, why? Why now? Why me?

It's to the point that I can't hold back. I've gotta know. "Why do you want to sell to me now?" I ask after he hands over a thick stack of papers. The contract his lawyer has drawn up. I'll be countering with a contract my lawyer will have put together, but there's no need to mention it at the moment. "After all this time, why me?"

Scott stares at me like I'm crazy. "Why not you? First,

you barrage me with calls and messages for months. Practically to the point of harassment. My plan was to ignore you. I wasn't ready to sell yet."

Swallowing hard, I rest my forearms on the edge of my desk, remaining as neutral as possible.

"Then you start dating my daughter and I wonder." His all-seeing gaze lands on me again, and I can tell he's trying to figure me out. "Are you using her to get to me? Tell me the truth."

Damn. I can't confess that was my original intention. It's not anymore. If I'm being truthful with myself, I can admit I'm halfway in love with her. More than halfway. It's just hard to come to grips with that sort of thing and admit it, especially to her father.

I haven't even told Marina how I feel. Yet.

"Would that change your price if I told you I was?" I ask, pretending to be the shrewd, ruthless businessman I used to be.

We glare at each other from across my desk, neither of us moving until he finally shakes his head.

"You're a bullshitter. It's written all over your face," he says.

"What are you talking about?"

"I can see that you're in love with Marina." I open my mouth to protest, but he narrows his gaze, silencing me with a single look that reminds me eerily of Marina. "Don't bother denying it. I know the two of you have been spending most of your time together."

He hasn't really been around lately, so I'm surprised he's noticed.

"I keep tabs on everything where my daughter is concerned." Another pointed look delivered by the man who I'm thinking might be my—gulp—father-in-law someday. How I can even think that way blows my mind. "That she even gave you a chance despite knowing what you wanted shows me she somehow saw beneath your surface."

Agreed. She's perceptive, my Marina. Smart and strong and beautiful and sexy as hell.

"I want to give her the bakery," I blurt, clamping my lips shut as soon as the words leave me. I hadn't meant to admit that yet.

"I think that's a good idea." Scott doesn't even flinch at my admission. Like he knew I'd planned it all along.

Strange. But perceptive. Kind of like his daughter.

"I want to keep it in your family. Give her the bakery as a gift, though she'll probably freak out if I offer it as a gift," I say, muttering the last few words.

"My daughter is full of pride. Sometimes it's foolish, sometimes it's not." Scott smiles. "I'm sure she'll be very appreciative of your generous gift."

"And wary," I add with a shake of my head. "She'll probably think there are strings attached to it."

"Are there?"

"Not at all." She loves the bakery. It's a part of her and her aunt, and I hate to see them lose it. "It means too much to her, and I can't let it slip out of her fingers."

"That right there is exactly why I'm ready to sell you the property. Though I can't deny there are financial reasons as well." The grimace on Scott Knight's face is unmistakable. "We've suffered these last few years. The economy hit the family businesses so hard, it's been a struggle to recuperate. I held on to the bakery and the buildings that surround it specifically for Marina and my sister-in-law for as long as I could. I know they both love it. I couldn't stand the thought of taking it away from them."

He just earned points for that admission.

"And now that you've confirmed that you want them to keep the bakery, I know my decision to sell to you was the right one." I'm guessing I just earned points as well.

"I want to take care of her, that's all," I say, stunned that I'd even admit such a thing to her father. But it's true. I want to provide her with what she wants, what she needs. There's something about her that makes me want to give her everything.

"That's an admirable trait," he says carefully.

Damn. I didn't mean to turn the conversation in this direction, but I guess I can't help it. Marina has slowly seeped into my world, and I can't imagine her out of it. "I'd appreciate it if you didn't say anything about me giving the bakery to Marina just yet," I say, because damn it, I want to be the one to tell her. "I want it to be a surprise."

"Of course. I completely understand." The smile on his face is small but there. "She'll be thrilled."

Hell, let's hope so.

Marina

"I missed you today." I snuggled closer to Gage, feeling like the clingy, simpering girlfriend, but for once I didn't care. I did miss him. I hate it when he goes to the city for business. I hate it worse when he's gone for a few days at a time, though that hasn't happened often. I love having him close.

Like right now, the both of us are naked in bed after an extremely sweaty bout of reunion sex. So we were apart for less than twenty-four hours; it's still considered reunion sex in my book.

Sighing, I turn my head and kiss his chest. Feeling his still-thundering heart beneath my lips. I've got it so bad for this man, it's ridiculous.

Ridiculously scary.

"I missed you too," he says, his deep voice gravelly. He's trailing his fingers up and down my arm, his touch soothing. Arousing. Closing my eyes, I get lost in the moment. Being with Gage helps me forget all my troubles. My nagging mother, my failing business, all of it slips away until I can only focus on Gage and how good he makes me feel.

"How was San Francisco?" We hadn't bothered with the preliminaries when I'd shown up on his doorstep not quite an hour ago. He'd taken my hand, dragged me inside, and proceeded to strip me of my clothing and kiss every bare inch of my skin.

"It was . . . fine."

Hmm. I glance up at him to see his eyes are closed, his brow furrowed. I wonder if he's keeping something from me.

"Who'd you meet with?"

"Investors. No one important," he answers quickly.

Tipping his head, he kisses my forehead, his lips lingering, making my eyes shut again. "I don't want to talk about business."

He's definitely hiding something. But what? I don't get it. Maybe he had a bad day and doesn't want to focus on it. Maybe he's in secret negotiations with someone and doesn't trust me enough to let me know what's going on.

Ouch. That hurts far more than I care to admit. I know we haven't been seeing each other very long, but I've become closer to Gage than any other human being on the planet. I didn't think this was possible. When I first learned of him, I hated him on sight, and I didn't even know him.

Now I'm falling for him. Scary.

"You should come with me sometime." When I don't say anything he continues. "To San Francisco. We can stay a few nights at the apartment I keep there."

"And what? Never leave the bed?" I tease.

He chuckles, then kisses my forehead again. "I could take you out."

"Maybe I don't want to go out." I tip my head back so I can see his handsome face. "Maybe I like keeping you all to myself."

Leaning in, he kisses me, soft and damp. "I like keeping you to myself, too."

"See? We don't need to go anywhere. We don't even have to leave this bed. We could stay here forever," I say.

He moves so fast I burst out laughing. He's over me, his hips pressed to mine, his growing erection nudging against my belly. Just like that he wants me.

And just like that, I want him too.

"Didn't we already do this?" I murmur before he kisses me deeply. Our tongues tangle, my brain empties, and I'm done with thinking. Talking.

All I can do is feel.

Feel his mouth on mine, already familiar yet delicious. The velvety glide of his tongue, the way his hands roam my body, the thrust of his cock against my belly reminding me he wants me. Again.

It's a heady, exhilarating sensation, knowing how much power I wield over Gage Emerson. He wants me always.

I feel the same way.

"You're probably tired," he whispers against my lips, one large hand cupping my breast, his thumb playing with my nipple.

I arch into his palm. "It's still early."

"And sore," he continues, rearing up so he's on his knees between my spread legs. He grips the base of his erection and brushes the head against my sex, making me gasp. "I sort of lost control with you earlier."

He'd pounded inside of me hard. My orgasm had been intense. But like the greedy woman I am, I want another one.

Now.

"I liked it," I murmur, reaching out so I can touch him. I race my hands over his chest, down his stomach, until I'm touching his cock and making him groan. "Grab a condom, Gage."

He wastes no time, reaching for the stash he keeps in

his bedside table and tearing one open. I watch in fascination as he rolls it on, loving how he moves, how he handles himself. He's a beautiful, sexy man and my heart literally fills with happiness knowing he's *my* man.

All mine.

"I wanna make this last," he whispers, sounding a little desperate as he grabs hold of my hips and flips us over so now I'm the one on top of him. "Give me a show, baby."

Smiling, I lower myself on him, until he's completely imbedded inside of me. He settles his hands on my waist, holding me there, his eyes glowing with some sort of unfamiliar emotion that makes my heart race.

He's looking at me like he can't get enough of me. And that's scary. Exciting.

Frightening.

Slowly, I start to move, trying to prolong it but already feeling anxious. He grips my ass, lifts up so he can take a nipple in his mouth and suck it, and I groan, tossing my head back as I slip my hands into his hair and hold him to me.

"You're beautiful," he whispers against my skin. "So goddamn beautiful I can't believe you're mine."

I feel the same way. The same exact way. I know my parents don't necessarily approve of us together. I know the way we met was sort of unusual. I didn't like him very much. I don't think he liked me either.

But the connection between us can't be denied. We're in so deep I don't think I ever want it to end. And I never think that way. I don't think Gage does either.

He leans back against the pillows, the satisfied smirk on his face downright arrogant as he watches me ride him. I increase my pace, gather my hair up in my hands and hold it there, sitting up straight so he can get that show he wants. Thrusting my chest out, I let go of my hair, shivering as the strands slide all over my breasts, tickling my hard, still-damp nipples. I shift forward, taking his cock deeper inside my body, and the agonized groan that leaves him makes me laugh.

"You're wicked," he murmurs, slipping a hand between our bodies so he can stroke my clit with his index finger.

It's my turn to gasp. "So are you."

"I want to watch you come." His touch firms, and I move faster, my entire body tingling with my impending orgasm. "Reach for it, baby."

Funny thing is I don't have to reach for it. He makes it so easy. His assured touch, the way he talks to me, looks at me: all of it sends me straight over the edge and into orgasmic bliss.

"Yeah, that's it," he says as I start to tremble, a little whimper escaping me. "Come for me, Marina."

I do. My entire body stills above his as my climax takes over. I moan his name, reaching out so I can grip his shoulders hard, and then he's coming as well, whispering my name against my hair as I collapse on top of him, the both of us shaking in each other's arms.

"Damn, woman," he mutters seconds, maybe minutes later, his hands gripping my butt once more, holding me close. Like he never wants to let me go.

"I know," I whisper, pressing my lips against his neck, tasting his delicious salty skin. "I feel the same way."

God. It would be so easy to fall in love with this man.

In fact, I think I'm already close to being there.

Chapter Thirteen

Marina

A LOT CAN change in a few weeks; heck, even a month. I was single and lonely, working my butt off day in and day out with little reward beyond growing a relationship with my aunt, which I cherish, but still. I'd watched the business I love slowly start to fail and it was eating at my very soul. The disappointment from my family—my ever-traveling, too-busy father and overprotective mother—was growing harder and harder to bear.

I had no friends. Many of them had moved away. Or I had no time to spend with the few friends I had.

Life had kind of sucked. I latched onto the fact that Gage Emerson was trying to buy out my family and ruin our lives. I went to that stupid little event more in the hopes of talking to him rather than conducting business, which had been my original intent. Maybe sling an insult or three at him, too, and then walk out, satisfied that I'd let the guy trying to take away my family legacy know I was onto him.

Well. We got the insult-slinging part right, at least.

Everything is completely different now. I have a friend, one I spend a lot of time with. Ivy Emerson and I made good on that San Francisco shopping trip and went last week. She helped me try on a ton of clothes, things I would never have looked twice at. I ended up buying a few things, not wanting to go beyond my self-imposed budget. She helped with that.

She helps with a lot of things.

Archer and I finalized the deal and Aunt Gina's desserts are in his hotel restaurants. Gina's thrilled. Archer's taken her completely under his wing. I'll be lucky to keep her with me at the bakery, what with the way he coddles her. I think Archer wants to steal her away from me.

My dad is still traveling a lot for business. My mom is still overprotective. I can't change them, I just have to learn how to live with them.

And then there's Gage.

I still can't quite define what's happening between us, but we're definitely . . . involved. I can't get enough of him. It seems he can't get enough of me either.

My entire life has changed for the better. A lot of it I owe to Gage. The very man who I believed was my enemy. He's introduced me to my newest friend. He helped me put together a business deal with Archer, his best friend. And he's made me . . .

Fall completely in love with him.

Just thinking about it makes me want to both jump for joy and throw up.

Especially now, what with the headache I have going on. I don't know what caused it, but I had to leave the bakery to take a little break. I couldn't deal.

"So you're going out with him tonight. Again."

Great. Talk about now being able to deal.

I turn to find my mother standing in my doorway, her arms crossed in front of her chest, her expression sour. She's reluctantly gone along with me dating Gage. Only lately has she piped up and vocalized her opinions. I think she's afraid I'm falling for him.

Too late.

"I am." I mirror her position, feeling defensive. Since my dad has been out of town so much doing God knows what, she's become even more of a meddler. I know I live at home, but I'm freaking twenty-three years old. I'm hardly here anyway. I spend quite a few nights at the little house Gage keeps here in St. Helena. I stay there sometimes even when he goes back to his place in San Francisco to conduct business. Hopefully, someday soon I'll go with him.

But with my obligation to the bakery, I can hardly leave. Before Gage came into my life, I had no reason to leave.

Now I want to be wherever Gage is. Silly, but true.

"Do you know why he was in San Francisco last week?" She drops her arms at her sides and strides into my room, her expression full of fierce determination. "Do you? Did your new boyfriend tell you about the meeting he had with your father?"

"Wait. What?" I blink at her, not sure I heard her right. "Daddy and Gage met?" And Gage never told me? I knew they were getting along and had discussed setting up an appointment to talk further, but Gage didn't tell me they'd talked in San Francisco.

She nods, the satisfaction on her face painful to witness. It's almost like she wants to hurt me with this news. "It's happening, Marina. Gage Emerson is buying the entire strip of buildings the Molina Corp owns on Main Street. They'll belong to him within the next sixty days as long as all the paperwork is processed in a timely manner and they hit no snags."

Sixty days. I can't believe he didn't tell me. I don't understand why he kept this from me. What was his motive? Was he afraid I'd freak out? I'm more upset he kept it a secret. I'd finally come to grips with the possibility of losing the bakery. This revelation is throwing me for a loop.

"He'll most likely close down the bakery since it's the only business within the strip that's still owned by us. Unless the two of you can come up with some sort of lease agreement together? I'm sure he'd be willing to *work* with you," she says snidely.

"Why do you hate him so much?" I ask, my voice quiet. Inside I'm reeling, devastated by Gage's betrayal. When exactly was he going to tell me about this? Never? Right before he shut down my bakery? It makes no sense.

My mother trying to tear me down doesn't make any sense either.

"I don't hate him. I dislike what he's done to us."

"Mom." I go to her, grabbing her hands and giving them a squeeze. "We had to sell. You and Dad both worry about your retirement, about everyone in the family ending up with nothing when we've all counted on the properties to earn us income. This way you'll have ready cash flow and won't have to worry so much."

"He stole your future," she says bitterly, jerking out of my touch. "That man you're dating and spending the night with stole everything from you! Don't you get it? You're our only daughter, you have no real prospects beyond the very man who's ruining your life, and you act like you're making the right choice! What in the world is wrong with you?"

I blink at her, shocked by her outburst. Mom doesn't have outbursts. She's always calm and cool and so very, very wise. I used to go to her all the time when I was younger for advice. She's great under pressure—the exception being when it comes to me and the choices I make.

"He's not stealing from me," I tell her. "Can't you see how this will help you guys? I'll be fine. I don't need the bakery." But I do. What will I do without it? Gina has a job lined up already. Archer is secretly trying to woo her. He's totally being a dirty rat, but can I fault him for it? No. And at least he tells me to my face.

Gage just keeps his secrets to himself and pretends everything's fine. So do I. But everything is definitely not fine. I don't know what I'm going to do with myself when I lose the bakery. There's no point in denying it now.

Autumn Harvest is done for.

"You needed to know," Mom says firmly, going to sit on the edge of my bed. "I can't stand that he's kept you in the dark. You need to come up with another plan."

"Like what?" I sit on the bed next to her, my mind too full trying to process everything.

"Break it off with him. Finish your time at the bakery until it closes. Then go to Italy and visit your cousins," she suggests hopefully. "You can have a nice three-month-long vacation there. Enjoy the sights. Meet new people."

Dread fills me. The trip to Italy is one all unmarried Italian girls make in the hope that they can find a husband. Either they end up staying there for the rest of their lives with their new husbands or they bring them home. I've seen a few cousins do this very thing. Only one came back, with a macho, irritating-as-hell Italian who refused to speak English and bossed her around all the time.

She eventually divorced him, not that anyone could blame her. Though her mama acted like she thought her daughter was going straight to hell.

Sometimes, I really despise being a part of such a traditional family.

"I'm not going to Italy," I say vehemently. She needs to know that suggestion can't even make its way onto the table.

"Fine. Break up with him. Find something else to do. Go work with Gina at the hotel. You need to do something. Unless you have no problem living here with us for the rest of your life, unmarried and miserable."

"Are you living in the stone ages? What in the world is

wrong with you?" I stand, glaring down at her. "You act like my being single and jobless is a kiss of death!"

She stares up at me pointedly, not saying a word.

She doesn't have to. I heard what I said. And it's slowly sinking in that yes, indeed, being single and jobless is the kiss of death.

For me.

Yet again, proving how life can change in an instant. I've gone from bad to fabulous to absolutely terrible.

All in the matter of approximately four weeks.

Gage

"I LOVE AUTUMN Harvest." Ivy sighs, scrolling through the photos of the bakery I just uploaded on my laptop from my phone. "But we can definitely spruce it up for her. I'm almost finished with Matt's job and have something lined up right after it, but I can do this on the side. The bakery and café already have good bones, so it won't be too difficult. I can put something together quick."

"I don't want some slapped-together job, Ivy," I warn her, scrolling through the photos of the bakery that's so much a part of Marina, I can't imagine her not working there.

The bakery I now own. The building I'm going to give her as a gift.

Right before I ask her to marry me.

"I still can't believe you're doing this." Ivy smiles at me, slowly shaking her head. "I never thought I'd see you fall, Gage. You were such a jackass about Archer and me getting together. And now look at you."

"Hey, I was trying to protect you. I know how Archer is. Was," I correct when she sends me a pointed look.

"And I know how you were. A workaholic stick-in-the-mud who only found pleasure with the many cars you purchased."

Jesus. She makes me sound like a total loser. "Thanks a lot," I mutter.

She nudges me. "I only say that because I'm your sister, and I can be brutally honest." Pausing, Ivy contemplates me. "Can I tell you something else?"

"Can I handle it?" I ask warily.

"Oh yeah." She smiles, her eyes going soft, almost misty. She's so damn sentimental lately, I don't know what's wrong with her. "Marina is so good for you. And you're good for her. I love seeing the two of you together. I'm so excited. And thankful I like her."

"Yeah?" An ache forms in my chest, making me grab my sister and pull her in for a hug. "Thanks, Ive. It means a lot to have your approval."

"You're welcome." She pulls away from me, pressing her hand against the side of my head. Her eyes are swimming with tears. "I'm so glad I get along with Marina. She's going to make a great sister-in-law."

"Why are you crying?" I catch a tear with my thumb as it slides down her cheek, worry consuming me. My sister doesn't cry much. She doesn't have reason to cry. Archer keeps her too damn happy for her to ever be sad.

"Don't worry about me." She waves a hand, sniffing loudly. "I'm just pregnant."

"What the hell?" I stare at her, overcome with . . . all

sorts of overwhelming emotions. Happiness. Shock. And plenty of murderous thoughts because holy hell, Archer impregnated my sister? I could kill him.

"Stop looking like you want to kill Archer." Reaching out, she grabs my hands, clasping them tightly in her own. "This is a good thing. We're going to have a baby." She sniffs, the tears streaming down her cheeks freely now. "I'm so ha-happy."

"You don't look or sound happy to me. Jesus, Ive, you're not even married yet! Mom's gonna have a cow."

Ivy burst out laughing, looking like a hysterical mess. Mascara-streaked tears line her face as she laughs. "You sound just like you did when we were kids."

"Well, it's true. She's going to flip. She's been working on your wedding for months." Years, probably, not that I'm going to say it. Our mom's been living for this moment and now Ivy's going to waddle down the aisle with a big ol' belly?

Yeah. That'll go over real well.

"We're bumping the wedding date up a few months. Mom already knows. So does Dad," she says.

"And Archer?"

Ivy rolls her eyes. "Of course, he knows. What, you think I'd leave the father of my baby as the last to know? I don't think so."

"No, you leave that honor to the uncle of your baby." I smooth her hair out of her eyes, feeling overprotective of my baby sister . . . who's going to have a baby. Holy hell, this is crazy.

"We haven't had a chance to talk, and you've been

so busy." She grabs hold of my arm, giving it a squeeze. "Don't tell Marina. I want to tell her, but I couldn't tell her if you didn't know."

I hug her again because I can't resist, kissing her forehead. "I'm so happy for you, Ive. Even happy for that bastard you're going to marry. I hope you know what you're getting into."

"I do." She smiles as she withdraws from my embrace. "No regrets. I'm the luckiest girl in the world."

I hope someday I can make Marina half as happy as Archer makes my sister.

I LEFT ARCHER and Ivy's house to head back to St. Helena and the bakery. I've been planning this surprise for Marina for weeks, in the midst of taking over the properties her family sold to me. I kept that from her too, despite Archer's incessant nagging that I was making a huge mistake.

But it wasn't because I'm trying to hurt her or close down the bakery without her knowledge. This is my gift to her, ensuring the bakery stays within her family, where it belongs. I've already started the process and the paperwork's being drawn up. I plan on eventually handing over the deed for the bakery to her.

Now I gotta figure out how to make this surprise announcement to her without freaking her completely out. I can't make too big of a deal about it. I need to tell Gina too. Ivy's in on it because she can't wait to help redesign the interior, her services free of charge, a gift to both me and Marina.

Marina's going to love it. So is Gina. Archer, not so much, because he's trying to steal Gina away from Marina every chance he can get.

Such a greedy jackass, though I can relate.

I enter the bakery, the familiar, delicious scent of bread baking hitting my senses, making my stomach rumble despite not really being hungry. I wave to Eli at the counter and head into the kitchen where I find Gina shedding her apron and hanging it on a wall hook.

"Well, well, look who the cat dragged in." She tsks and shakes her head. "How you doing, Pretty Boy?"

Thank God I've been upgraded from Boy Toy. She still calls Archer Rat Boy, which he deserves. "I'm great. Where's Marina?"

"Not in. She went home earlier, said she didn't feel well."

I frown. She never let me know. "Is she all right?" I'm extra sensitive, I guess, because of my sister's major announcement, and I wonder: What would that be like, being with Marina? Getting her pregnant, watching her body shift and change, her belly full of my baby?

That strange ache seems to strangle my heart again, and I rub at my chest absently, wondering what the hell is wrong with me.

You're in love, you idiot. You'd do anything for that woman constantly in your thoughts.

"I'll call her," I say, watching as Gina gathers her purse from the closet she keeps it in and her sweater. "Mind if I go hang out in her office for a bit so I can call her in there?" I'm going to grab a few old brochures I know she keeps stashed in her bookshelf and give them to a marketing specialist I've worked with in the past. I plan on having some new materials created, along with a new logo.

Oh yeah, I have lots of plans. And all of them are going to blow Marina's mind. Make her love me that much more.

I wander into her office, searching her tiny bookshelf, plucking first one, then a few other old advertising pieces I can find. Two brochures, a couple of postcards, all of it's good to show the graphic designer.

Sitting behind her desk, I call her on my cell but get no answer. Send her a text asking if she's feeling okay, but again, no reply. Grabbing the brochures, I stack them neatly atop the desk, the edge of the cardstock nudging her mouse, and her monitor lights up, the security business site I know she uses at the bakery coming up on screen.

Squinting, I look at the black and white, slightly fuzzy image, noticing that it's a man, bent over . . . a woman? I see that the image is paused; this is actual footage taken within the bakery, and when I hit play, it all becomes too clear what I'm looking at.

That's me. And Marina. Having sex in the kitchen that first night we attacked each other.

I run a hand through my hair, glancing around like someone's going to walk up on me at any minute and discover what I'm looking at. I'm completely blown away. I can't believe Marina's kept this on her computer for . . . what? Her viewing pleasure? It happened over a month ago. We've had plenty of sex since then. Better sex, infinitely more satisfying sex. Every time we come together, it's better and better between us. We're lucky.

And now I'm . . . shocked, seeing us on her computer screen, me pounding inside of her, her head thrown back, her long legs wound tight around me as she clutches my shoulders with her hands. There's no sound, but I don't need to hear it to remember. She's panting hot, encouraging words, and I'm sliding so deep inside her I groan her name, ready to give in to the urge and let my orgasm take over.

Damn. It's sort of hot, seeing us together like this. Maybe I can understand why she kept it, but still. She should've let me see this. At the very least told me about it. I hit pause, catching her at a particularly good angle. The expression on her face tells me she's pretty damn close to orgasm.

I really like seeing that expression on her face, but live and in person. Not on a video I happen to discover hidden away on her computer. Why would she keep it? Was she hoping to somehow use it against me if I did her wrong? I've gone out with vindictive women before. Women out to get me before I got them, always on the defense when I never thought that way in the first place.

"What are you doing?"

I glance up to find Marina standing just inside her office, her eyes bloodshot, her expression tight. She looks terrible.

So, so sad.

Pushing away from her desk, I go to her, but she dodges

me at the last minute. "What happened? Are you okay?" I ask, worry consuming me. She's acting odd. "Gina said you went home because you weren't feeling well."

"I'm fine. Really." She runs a hand over her head, messing up her hair rather than fixing it. She's looking at me like she doesn't quite know what to do with me. "I had a headache. So I went home. Had an interesting conversation with my mother too. Let me tell you, it didn't help with my headache whatsoever. I'd say after her news, it's even worse. I had to get out of there, so I came back here."

My heart skips over itself. Shit. "What did you two talk about?" I ask, afraid to hear her answer.

"Oh, you know. She's worried I'm going to die a bitter, single, *jobless* old woman." One delicate brow rises and I know exactly what she's referring to.

Double shit. This is not the way I wanted her to find out.

"Marina," I start, and she holds up her hand, silencing me.

"I don't want to hear your excuses," she says quietly, her expression flat, her eyes dim. "Tell me the truth. When were you going to let me know huh, Gage? *When*?"

She knows. I'd asked her father to keep it a secret so I could tell her she's not losing the bakery and I withheld the information too long. Now she's pissed. "It's not what you think—" I start, but she cuts me off.

"Then what am I supposed to think? I don't understand how you can keep something so incredibly important from me. Who are you? Why would you do this? The bakery closing changes everything, my entire life! I'll have nothing. No job, no nothing. All because of you." She rushes toward me, shoving at my chest so hard I take a step back, shocked at the force behind her push. "You're evil."

Wait. Her dad didn't tell her about the bakery. This is even worse. She thinks I'm trying to shut her down. "Marina—"

"Shut up. You're a liar. Withholding information is just as bad as lying. I can't believe you would do this to me. I thought you lo . . ." She clamps her lips shut, closing her eyes and slowly shaking her head.

"Let me explain myself. It's not what you think," I start, but she opens her eyes and glares at me.

"Don't bother trying to explain, Gage. You got what you wanted. I knew you wanted to buy those buildings from the start, so I don't know why I'm so surprised or hurt. I guess I got too caught up."

Damn it. She's not even listening to me. "What about *your* secret?" I toss out, my voice flat.

Her eyes widen, tears sparkling in them. Damn it, just the sight of them makes my chest ache. "What secret?"

I fold my arms across my chest, leaning against the edge of her desk. If she won't even listen to me, then I need to get the truth out of her regarding the security tape. It's weird that she never mentioned it. "I think you might know what I'm talking about."

Chapter Fourteen

Marina

I HAVE ABSOLUTELY no idea what he's talking about. I'm not the secret-keeper in this relationship. He is.

And boy is his secret a doozy, one that's going to change my life forever.

He acts like it's no big deal.

"Stop playing games," I murmur, letting my anger fuel me. He's propped against my desk, his arms crossed in front of his chest, his biceps straining against his long-sleeved shirt, but I ignore the way my body responds to his. He always makes me feel this way. Hungry, desperate, needy. All for him.

I'm too mad. Angry sex with Gage is amazing—we've indulged a few times because we're sort of sick and twisted like that—but not like this. Not with this sort of horrible betrayal.

He's taken it too far.

"I saw what you keep on your computer." He waves his hand toward the monitor. "I had no idea we made a porn video, Marina. Wish you would've told me. Do you plan on selling it now that you know what a jerk I really am? Distributing it online so it can make the rounds? Maybe earn a few million hits on YouTube?"

Gasping, I round the desk, staring at the screen where the video is paused. There we are in black and white. I can see my naked legs wrapped around him, his body hovering over mine, my arms around his neck. I minimize the screen, glancing up to find him studying me, his expression downright deadly.

"Why do you have that on your computer?" he asks, his voice scary quiet. "It makes no sense for you to keep it this long. Unless you did it on purpose so you could use it against me."

I'm in complete shock. Does he really think that low of me? What sort of women did he date in his past? "I . . . the morning after the encounter in the kitchen, kids smashed the pumpkins we had around the front door." I'm going to tell him the entire story, even if it kills me. "So I checked the videos from the night before and saw the kids but couldn't identify them."

"Okay," he says slowly, probably wondering why I'm telling him all this.

But there is a point to my story. "Then I clicked through, checking out all the cameras we have and I saw this. Us." Closing my eyes, I breathe deep, searching for strength. I can't believe I'm the one who has to explain myself when *he's* the one who kept the worst secret ever.

I open my eyes and continue. "I—liked watching it. I was so confused after what happened between us. How could I hate someone and want him, all at the same time? You drove me crazy. Keeping this video was my way of . . . holding on to something that has sentimental value, you know?"

"A video of us fucking in your kitchen has sentimental value?" He laughs and shakes his head. "That's just great."

"I refuse to let you make me feel guilty. I had it up on my computer because I was going to delete it." I don't know why I held onto it so long. Earlier I'd brought it back up, ready to delete when my mom called. I pushed away from my computer, talked to her a bit, felt the headache come on, and then left, forgetting all about it. "I realized it probably wasn't smart, having a video of us. What if it fell into the wrong hands?"

"No shit. Not one of your most brilliant moves, Marina." He snorts, shaking his head.

Ah, there's the old Gage. The one I want to slap across the face for saying such shitty, hurtful things. I stand, slapping my hands against the edge of the desk. "Don't try and make this all about what I've done to you. It's minor compared to what you've done and you know it. You're the one who bought out my dad and Molina Corp. Why didn't you tell me? How long were you going to wait? I deserved to know, Gage."

He glares at me, his green eyes cold. Hard. "You really think I would purposely keep this from you so I could *hurt* you, Marina? After everything we've gone through, everything we've experienced this last month? You don't know me at all, do you?"

I shrug, trying to blow it off. I have no idea what's real and what's not anymore. I don't care how gutted he sounds. As hard as it is for me to realize, I don't think I can trust him. "I don't know. It's only been a month. What could I expect from you?"

It's Gage's turn to rush me, coming round the desk so he's standing in front of me, his hands clasping my upper arms, shaking me as if he can knock some sense into me. "I'm in love with you, damn it. I wanted to show you how I felt by giving you the goddamn deed to this place. I was going to give it to you as a surprise and Ivy was going to redecorate the café. I was putting together an advertising plan and everything. Anything you wanted for this place, I would've given you."

I gape at him, shock rendering me completely still. He was going to give me the deed? As a gift? And have his sister redecorate the café? I can't . . . oh my God. I'm such a jerk. "Why didn't you tell me though? You should've. My mom took great pleasure in being the first one to deliver the news."

I'm still so angry at him. I don't know if I'll ever feel the same way about him again. His words alone nearly destroyed me.

Now that I know he planned all of this? I don't know what to think. What to do.

How to react.

"Yeah, I know. I fucked up. Archer said I should tell you. So did Ivy. But I wanted it to be a surprise. It was a risky move, and look. I really ruined it now." He laughs, sounding borderline hysterical, and I want to go to him. Comfort him. Tell him everything's going to be okay.

But I can't. It still feels like a betrayal, just like me keeping the video of our first sexual encounter feels like a betrayal to him.

Now he talks about his plans in the past tense. Like I ruined my chances to be with him. Work with him.

Love him.

"You're mad at me, aren't you." It's not a question. He sounds so defeated, my heart is breaking for him. For me. My anger is slowly evaporating, turning more on my mother, which I know is pointless. She's my mom. I won't be angry with her forever.

Gage hangs his head, closing his eyes as he breathes deep. "I'm so sorry, Marina. I shouldn't have done it like this. I made a mistake. I know you can't trust me, but now I'm starting to wonder if I can't trust you either."

"Do you mean because of the video?" I ask him, my voice barely above a whisper. I can't believe it. He's that mad about the video?

"Yeah." He nods, opening his eyes to stare at me. "You should've told me."

"Right back at you," I automatically say.

We stand in front of each other, the both of us silent, as if we're waiting for the other to say something. Anything.

But neither of us do.

Finally he turns and leaves without another word. Just strides out of my office like I never existed and walks right out of my life.

Only after he's gone do I collapse into my chair, resting my head on my desk as I sob into the pile of overdue invoices that still haunt me.

Gage

"YOU'RE STILL GOING through with it." Archer sounds incredulous.

"I am," I mutter, watching the company I hired repaint the café walls. "She's given up on this place, but I won't."

Two weeks after our big blowup, she hung the closed sign in the door and shut down Autumn Harvest for good. I was stunned. Marina's no quitter. I have no idea what's come over her, and since she refuses to see me, I guess I'll never find out.

Luckily enough she still talks to Ivy, who keeps me fully informed. She says Marina's considering going back to school so she can get her master's degree. But this time, she'd like to travel elsewhere. Maybe go to an East Coast school. Start over with a fresh new life. I know what she's really referring to. She'd rather start over.

Without me.

I've taken over the business completely. Hell, I own it, so I can do whatever I want to it, right? I had new appliances installed, including a new oven, and I consulted Gina as to which I should purchase.

When I got off the phone with her, she called me Smart Boy—and in the same breath, a total dumbass. I'd reached both the pinnacle of approval and the absolute bottom of disappointment, all at once with Aunt Gina.

"It's going to look pretty damn amazing," Archer says,

glancing around the room, which is still under a massive construction overhaul. "Ivy's been keeping me posted."

"How's she feeling?" We're both a pair of overprotective males watching out for her and I know she hates it. Yet she likes it too, all at the same time.

"Feeling a little better, not so queasy. The morning sickness is what's taking her down so hard. Plus she's so tired."

"I know. She tried to get me to let her come for this, but I told her no way. I didn't want her inhaling the fumes," I say.

"Good call." Archer exhales loudly before he turns to me. "Have you spoken to her?"

"Who? Ivy?"

"No, jackass. Marina. When was the last time you talked to her?"

"Not since we split." I shrug, acting like it's no big deal, but not having her as a part of my life feels like I'm missing a piece of me.

I fucking hate it.

"Seriously? And I thought *I* was stubborn." He shakes his head, looking ready to launch into a big ol' speech, and I brace myself. "Look, you need to go to her and tell her you're sorry. Ivy goes and sees her all the time and she says she's miserable."

"She never tells me that. Ivy acts like Marina's just fine."

"Yeah well, I think she's trying to spare your feelings or worry or whatever. She's not fine. She's a wreck and plans on leaving to go to college across the country so she can escape her mother. She misses you. Not that you're supposed to know that." Archer points at me.

I keep my expression blank. "I have no idea what you're talking about."

"Good answer. I just . . . I can't stand to see the two of you suffer. I know she did wrong and you did wrong." I never told him exactly what happened, only that Marina kept something very important from me as well. The both of us weren't perfect in this situation. I probably overreacted, but I've been with some bat-shit-crazy women in the past who would've probably used a sex tape against me to get whatever they wanted.

Meaning I've dated some pretty awful women, women who weren't worthy of cleaning Marina's toilet, let alone be in the same league as her.

"You can't keep this up," Archer continues when I don't say anything. "It's killing you both. You're a wreck without her. Throwing yourself into your work, fixing up her bakery as some sort of homage to her? I mean, what the hell are you doing?"

"I want to do this. For her, whether she appreciates it or not."

"Right," Archer deadpans. "You're crazy."

Slowly I nod, knowing I sound crazy, but I'm not changing my mind. "This bakery belongs to Marina. It's hers, no questions. And if she doesn't want it, then I fully plan on giving it to Gina. This place needs to stay in the Molina and Knight family. It belongs with them."

A smile spreads across Archer's face. "You do have a heart, don't you?"

"Shut up." I shove at his shoulder. "Don't tell anyone. I don't want it getting out."

I miss her. My body, my mind, my heart, they all ache without Marina in my life. I refuse to go to her though. Not until I have something to show her. Something that will prove my love to her and let her know without a doubt that I will do anything, and I mean *anything* for her.

Like revamp her business. From the kitchen to the front end of the store, to the new computer and ordering systems that are going to be installed within the next few days, everything's state of the art. Top notch.

My girl deserves the absolute best.

"You're also a sap. You still plan on presenting the bakery to her, right?"

"As long as Ivy's still bringing Marina to the grand re-opening, then yeah. I'm doing it." No one can say I didn't go for it with this, now can they?

"She is. Ivy told me. Marina's thrilled that Ivy's pregnant," Archer informs me.

"I bet," I murmur, not sure what to think. Why does he tell me stuff like this? Only makes me miss her more.

And damn, do I miss her. It's only been a few weeks but it feels like years. I miss her voice, her smile, the way she yells at me when I make her angry. The whispery little moans that escape her when I make her come. I miss her scent, the way she likes to cook my dinner, how she snuggles up against my back when we sleep together.

I miss everything about her. I want her back in my life.

Within the next two weeks, I'm hoping like crazy I can make it that happen.

Once and for all.

Chapter Fifteen

Two weeks later

Marina

"I DON'T WANT to go," I moan, hiding my head beneath the pillows. It's way too early for me to have to deal with this. Ever since Ivy's become pregnant, she's been on a tear. She turned into a total bossy little thing who has no problem pushing people into doing stuff they normally would never do.

"Tough shit." Ivy yanks the sheet off me, making me shriek. Damn, the air is cold. Almost as cold and unfeeling as she is. "We're going to this all-day spa and we're going to love it, even if it kills us."

That she's forcing me to go to a spa shows how ridiculous I am. I'm the biggest baby ever. Since I shut down the bakery and café, I've become a total recluse, barely getting out of my pajamas, let alone going to see anyone. I'd rather wallow in my misery.

"I don't want to be buffed and pampered," I whimper as I slide out of bed, shuffling toward my bathroom. Ivy's already dressed and looks adorable, her growing baby belly so cute everyone wants to touch it, which drives her nuts. She's not a big fan of complete strangers touching her and asking when the baby is due. I've even witnessed her pretending she has no clue what they're talking about.

That always freaks them out.

I force myself into the shower, perking up considerably once I stand beneath the hot spray of water for a solid ten minutes. I emerge from the bathroom a little over twenty minutes later to find the smell of coffee calling to me.

Dang. I should ask Ivy to move in with me.

We sip coffee and talk, Ivy telling me about Archer wanting to take her to Hawaii before the baby is born and how she really doesn't want to go. I tell her she's crazy, they need to savor all the alone time they can get before that baby comes and totally changes their lives.

Ivy agrees.

We're finally on the road in Ivy's car, ready to head to the spa resort when she turns toward St. Helena, a neutral expression on her face.

"Where are you going?" I ask her, my voice quiet, my thoughts a jumbled-up mess.

I miss Gage. My mom is thrilled we're finished and wants to talk about what a jerk he is, but I told her any discussion about Gage is off limits. Dad leaves me alone because he knows I'm heartbroken and Mom gave him the same talk I gave her.

No talk of Gage in the house. Ever.

But I want to talk about Gage. How happy he made me. How passionate we were together, both in bed and out of it. He made me think, he made me want to achieve something. Anything. He made me strong.

And now I feel weak and lonely without him.

"I needed to pick up something first," she says vaguely, waving her hand.

Huh. I don't like where this is going. I remain calm, though, and notice the colorful bunches of balloons hanging in front of . . . the bakery.

A giant crowd of people are waiting outside, and I see my familiar chalkboard easel, the words GRAND REOPEN-ING written in bold script across the front of it.

No way. I had no clue the bakery was being reopened. Gage sure did move fast.

And doesn't that leave a bitter taste in my mouth.

Ivy drives by the bakery slowly, coming almost to a complete stop so I can see everything. God, she's obvious. "I wonder what's going on in there?" she asks innocently.

I don't know how she can keep a straight face. "Gee, I don't know, Ivy. Maybe we should go inside and see what's going on."

"That's perfect!" She claps her hands together and then parks the car. She's practically leading me by the hand toward the café, and my feet are dragging. I so don't want to go in there. I don't want to see the new owners, though I have my suspicions the only owner is Gage.

Still. I don't want to deal with this. Deal with him.

Not only is the outside of the café and bakery overflowing with people waiting in line to get in, but the inside of the café is packed too. Somehow, the determined pregnant lady gets us inside and I'm immediately shocked by all the changes.

The entire interior has been repainted, and Gage ordered all new tables and chairs, giving the location a cleaner, simpler feel. A new glass case has been installed, as well as new countertops, and I can't help but gape at everything, too stunned to study any of it for too long for fear it'll up and disappear.

"The kitchen is revamped too," Ivy says close to my ear so I can hear her. The chattering crowd is absolutely deafening. "You should go check it out. There's all state-of-the-art appliances. Your aunt is in seventh heaven."

"Wait a minute. Gina is working here?"

"How do you think they're able to have the open house if they have no one here to bake all the goodies? Yes, she still works here. And she's loving every minute of it, despite Archer wanting to steal her away. Not that I can talk about it." She clamps her lips shut and does the universal sign for lock-them-up-and-throw-away-the-key. "Archer will kill me if he finds out I told you he's desperate to take Gina."

Yeah right. Like Archer would ever lay a hand on Ivy. "Take me to the kitchen," I tell her, needing her with me so I won't have to confront any of my fears—as in Gage—alone.

She escorts me back there, and the closer we get to

that swinging door, the more heavily I lean on her. My heart is racing double time, my feet feeling like they have lead weights on top of them, and I stop just before we go through the door so I can look at her.

"There's no spa day planned, is there?"

"This is it." She throws her arms out, a silly smile on her face for a moment before it slowly starts to fade. "I hate nothing more than seeing my two favorite people in the entire world, besides the man I'm going to marry, so miserable without each other."

I hang my head, breathing deep. I hate that we're so miserable too.

"You two need to talk and listen to each other. He never meant to hurt you, Marina. I hope you've finally realized that."

Slowly I nod, not wanting her to see me. I feel weak and blink back the tears that are threatening to spill.

Ivy moves in closer so she can whisper in my ear. "Let him spoil you. He's so in love with you it's disgusting. He would do anything to make you happy." With a gentle shove, she pushes me through the swinging door, and I lose my footing, sending me nearly sprawling as I tumble inside the kitchen.

My gaze goes wide as I drink everything in. The layout is the same, but the appliances are all brand new. Big, gorgeous, stainless steel—and all top of the line.

That had to have cost a pretty penny.

"You like it?"

I whirl around with a gasp to find Gage standing before me, clad in an Autumn Harvest T-shirt, much like the one I used to wear, and a pair of jeans. He looks delicious, tired, happy, sad, and worried.

I can relate to him on every single thing except the delicious part. I'm not feeling very delicious.

"It's beautiful, Gage," I whisper, bracing myself when he approaches me.

"I did it for you." He reaches for my hands and holds them loosely in his. "I did it all for you. The revamp of everything, the grand reopening, all the new advertising materials, all for my girl. The local paper is going to do a write-up about you too. You'll be famous."

I'm only stuck on a few choice words he mentioned in that pretty speech. God, I missed him so much. Having him in front of me, so handsome but looking so unsure, makes my heart swell with overwhelming emotion for him. "Your girl?"

Slowly he nods, his fingers tightening around mine. "You're mine. Whether we're together or apart, I know it. I think you know it too." He takes a deep breath and exhales slowly. "I've been miserable without you in my life. I need you, Marina. I need you by my side, working with me, laughing with me. Loving me." His eyes glow as he steps closer, and I hold my breath, waiting for him to say something more. "Tell me you still feel the same."

Gage

I WAIT WITH near unbearable anticipation to hear what she has to say. Ivy bringing her here to see the bakery and me is a good sign. If she hated me, she wouldn't have come in.

At the moment, I'm looking for any sort of positive sign—I'm that desperate.

"What you've done here is so beautiful." She smiles at me, her eyes shiny with unshed tears. "Thank you. I don't deserve this."

Ah, that's where she's wrong. She deserves all of this and more. So much more. "I know we've gone through our ups and downs. We've both made some dumb choices. But I don't ever, ever regret meeting you. Arguing with you. Having angry sex with you." My voice lowers. "Falling in love with you."

Her lips part, a shaky exhalation leaving her, and I pull her in, slipping my arms around her waist so I can crush her to me. I never want to let her go.

"Oh, Gage." She presses her face against my chest and begins to cry, leaving me feeling helpless by her tears.

"Don't cry," I whisper against her hair as I stroke it with my fingers. "I love you."

"I love you too," she sobs into my shirt.

I smile despite her tears. What she just said is a good thing. A very, very good thing. "I want you to marry me," I whisper close to her ear.

She withdraws from my embrace but I don't let her go too far. "What did you say?"

"I want you to marry me. We'll live here in St. Helena in the little house I'm having renovated and we'll keep the San Francisco house for all the cars. They all can't fit here. We'll only have a single-car garage," I say, earning a smile.

"Only if you promise to build a garage so we can keep

a few of your cars here. I'd want to take them out for a test drive." She nibbles on her bottom lip, driving me wild just watching at her. "You know. Just for . . . fun."

Ah, damn this woman. She is just perfect for me in every way. "You've got it. Whatever you want," I vow.

"What about your real estate business?"

"I can do that from here." I have been for almost two months and everything's worked out fine. "We're not too far from the city so I can drive in when needed. It'll all work out. As long as we have each other, we can make it work."

She smiles up at me, her pretty eyes sparkling at me. "What about that proposal you mentioned."

I frown. "Proposal?"

Marina frowns back. "Yes, you know. The one where you mentioned marriage?"

"Ahh." I'm a complete bonehead. Reaching inside my front pocket, I pull out a small box and hand it to her. "Here you go."

She opens the box with shaking fingers, a small gasp escaping her when she sees the glittering two-carat diamond nestled inside. "It's too big," she immediately protests, glaring at me.

"It's perfect." Taking the box from her, I withdraw the ring and grab her left hand, sliding the solitaire onto her ring finger. It fits. "You're perfect." I kiss the tip of her nose.

"Hmm. I think you're the one who's perfect." Leaning up on tiptoe, she kisses me, turning it instantly deep and hot. She sways against me, I grab hold of her hips and let myself become acquainted with her delicious, persistent lips and tongue when I hear a voice clearing nearby.

Popping my eyes open, I find Gina starting at us, her expression irritable. "You two kids made up then?"

Marina turns within my embrace, her back to my front as I wrap my arms around her waist. She settles her arms over mine, our fingers interlaced, her head resting against my chest. I've never felt this content. "We have," she admits dreamily. "Gage asked me to marry him."

"And you said yes."

She nods her confirmation.

"What about your parents?"

I feel her stiffen and squeeze her closer, willing her to relax. She finally does. "I think I can convince them to come around. Dad is more agreeable then Mom," Marina says.

"Well, you have your work cut out for you then, don't you, Pretty Boy?"

I inwardly groan at her choice of nickname. "So we're back to Pretty Boy?"

"Well, you sure are pretty with that shit-eating grin on your face now that you've got your woman back in your arms." Gina smiles and tilts her head toward the café. "You two need to get out there. Everyone wants to talk to you."

"Really?" Marina asks incredulously.

"Really," I say, kissing her temple. "They all know I did this for you."

"How come I was kept in the dark?" She pouts.

"You did that by choice, by becoming a total recluse,"

I tease, though it hurts me too. I hate that I made her feel so bad she could hardly drag herself out of bed.

She turns so she's facing me once more. We promise Gina we'll be out there in a few minutes just as she exits the kitchen.

"I am the luckiest woman in the world," Marina sighs against my lips before she starts kissing me again.

Damn it. She keeps this up, and we'll test out that new desk I had installed in the office. See if it's as sturdy as it appears. I set her away from me instead. "Later. Right now, we need to go greet our guests."

More mock pouting. Damn, her lips are luscious. Unable to resist, I drop a kiss on her forehead, her nose, lingering on those delicious lips. "Let's go out there and tell them our good news. You can show off your ring."

"Maybe I want to stay back here with you instead." A wicked gleam lights her eyes. "If there weren't so many people out there I'd suggest we reenact the first time we fooled around in the kitchen."

Damn. This woman blows my mind constantly. "You're out of control. Don't you still have the video? We can watch it later."

That wicked glow shines brighter. "I do still have it."

I drop a kiss on her nose. "Maybe we should make another one sometime." I can't even believe I made the suggestion, but that's how far gone I am for this woman. "Now come on, let's go talk to your customers."

"Gage." She stops me before I start out to the café front, a frown on her face. "So does our engagement mean you lost the bet?"

I frown, realization dawning as soon as I hear the words. "You know about the bet?"

Slowly she nods, nibbling on her lower lip. "Ivy told me a while ago, one night when we were hanging out. She said I had a right to know."

"And you're not mad?" I remember how Ivy had reacted. Not a pretty sight.

"Of course not. I wish you would've told me about it sooner." She loops her arms around my neck. "I would've helped you win."

Damn. More confirmation of just how perfect she is for me.

Gently pushing her away, I take her hand and we exit the kitchen, immediately greeted by the wild applause and celebratory shouts from our neighbors and customers. I even recognize a few friends in the crowd, though I hadn't noticed them before. The both of us step back, overwhelmed by the response, and she grins up at me, squeezing my hand.

My heart expands in my chest, filling up so much space, I'm almost afraid I can't breathe.

But that's okay. As long as I have Marina by my side, we can get through anything.

Together.

Don't miss how this million-dollar bet got started . . .
Keep reading for an excerpt from Book One in
Monica Murphy's sexy
Billionaire Bachelors Club series

CRAVE

Now available from Avon Impulse.

An Excerpt from

CRAVE

Ivy

A KNOCK SOUNDS at the door and I jump, grabbing the robe off the hook with lightning speed. Throwing it on, I approach, figuring it's Gage ready to tell me something lame before he goes to bed. He's always been a little over-protective, so he's probably just checking up on me.

"I'm fine, Gage. Really," I say as I open the door, stunned silent when I see who's standing before me.

"Really?" Archer raises a brow, one hand in his pants pocket, the other clutching an article of clothing. "Why wouldn't you be anything *but* fine?"

Oh. Shit. He should so not be standing in front of me right now. "What are you doing here?" I whisper, glancing over his shoulder to thankfully see Gage's door is closed.

"Making sure you're comfortable." He thrusts his hand out toward me. "I brought you something."

I'm ultra-aware of the fact that beneath the terry cloth, I'm wearing absolutely nothing. The impulse to untie the sash and let the robe drop to my feet just to see Archer's reaction is near overwhelming.

But I keep it under control. For now.

"What is this?" I take the wadded-up fabric from his hand, our fingers accidentally brushing, and heat rushes through me at first contact.

"One of my T-shirts." He shrugs those broad shoulders, which are still encased in fine white cotton. "I know you didn't have anything to wear to . . . bed. Thought I could offer you this."

His eyes darken at the word *bed* and my knees wobble. Good lord, what this man is doing to me is so completely foreign, I'm not quite sure how to react.

"Um, thanks. I appreciate it." The T-shirt is soft, the fabric thin, as if it's been worn plenty of times, and I have the sudden urge to hold it to my nose and inhale. See if I can somehow smell his scent lingering in the fabric.

The man is clearly turning me into a freak of epic proportions.

"You're welcome." He leans his tall body against the doorframe, looking sleepy and rumpled and way too sexy for words. I want to grab his hand and yank him into my room.

Wait, no I don't. That's a bad—terrible—idea.

Liar.

"Is that all then?" I ask, because we don't need to be standing here having this conversation. First, my brother could find us and start in again on what a mistake we are. Second, I'm growing increasingly uncomfortable with the fact that I'm completely naked beneath the robe. Third, I'm still contemplating shedding the robe and showing Archer just how naked I am.

"Yeah. Guess so." His voice is rough and he pushes away from the doorframe. "Well. Good night."

"Good night," I whisper, but I don't shut the door. I don't move.

Neither does he.

"Ivy . . ." His voice trails off and he clears his throat, looking uncomfortable. Which is hot. Oh my God, everything he does is hot and I decide to give in to my impulses, because screw it.

I want him.

Archer

LIKE AN IDIOT, I can't come up with anything to say. It's like my throat is clogged, and I can hardly force a sound out, what with Ivy standing before me, her long, wavy, dark hair tumbling past her shoulders, her slender body engulfed in the thick white robe I keep for guests. The very same type of robe we provide at Hush.

But then she does something so surprising—so amazingly awesome—I'm momentarily dumbfounded by the sight.

Her slender hands go for the belt of the robe and she undoes it quickly, the fabric parting, revealing bare skin. Completely bare skin.

Holy shit. She's naked. And she just dumped the robe

onto the ground so she's standing in front of me. Again, I must stress, *naked*.

My mouth drops open, a rough sound coming from low in my throat. Damn, she's gorgeous. All long legs and curvy waist and hips and full breasts topped with pretty pink nipples. I'm completely entranced for a long, agonizing moment. All I can do is gape at her.

"Well, are you just going to stand there and wait for my brother to come back out and find us like this or are you going to come inside my room?"

*Matt DeLuca may be the last man
standing. Can he win this bet?
Or will a sexy brunette steal away his win . . . and
his heart?
Continue reading for a sneak peek at the final
book in Monica Murphy's hot
Billionaire Bachelors Club series*

SAVOR

Coming in January 2014 from Avon Impulse.

An Excerpt from

SAVOR

Bryn

"I SHOULDN'T DO THIS." He's coming right at me, one determined step after another, and I slowly start to back up, fear and excitement bubbling up inside me, making it hard to think clearly.

"Shouldn't do what?"

I lift my chin, my gaze meeting his, and I see all the turbulent, confusing emotions in his eyes, the grim set of his jaw and usually lush mouth. The man means business—what sort of business I'm not exactly sure, but I can take a guess. Increasing my pace, I take hurried backward steps to get away from all that handsome intensity coming at me until my butt meets the wall.

I'm trapped. And in the best possible place too.

"You've been driving me fucking crazy all night," he practically growls, stopping just in front of me.

I have? I want to ask, but I keep my lips clamped tight. He never seems to notice me, not that I ever really want him to. Or at least, that's what I tell myself. That sort of thing usually brings too much unwanted attention. I've dealt with that sort of trouble before, and it nearly destroyed me.

The more time I spend with my boss though, the more I want him to see me. Really see me as a woman. Not the dependable, efficiently organized Miss James who makes his life so much easier.

I want Matt to see me as a woman. A woman he wants. *Playing with fire . . .*

The thought floating through my brain is apt, considering the potent heat in Matt's gaze.

"I don't understand how I could be, considering I've done nothing but work my tail off the entire evening," I retort, wincing the moment the words leave me. I blame my mounting frustration over our situation. I'm tired, I've done nothing but live and breathe this winery opening for the last few weeks, and I'm ready to go home and crawl into bed. Pull the covers over my head and sleep for a month.

But if a certain someone wanted to join me in my bed, there wouldn't be any sleeping involved. Just plenty of nakedness and kissing and hot, delicious sex . . .

My entire body flushes at the thought.

"And I appreciate you working that pretty tail of yours off for me. Though I'd hate to see it go," he drawls, his gaze dropping low. Like he's actually trying to check out my backside. His flirtatious tone shocks me, rendering me still.

Our relationship isn't like this. Strictly professional is how Matt and I keep it between us. But that last remark was most definitely what I would consider flirting. And the way he's looking at me . . .

Oh. My.

My cheeks warm when he stops directly in front of me. I can feel his body heat, smell his intoxicating scent, and I press my lips together to keep from saying something really stupid.

God, I want you. So bad my entire body aches for your touch.

Yeah. I sound like those romance novels I used to devour when I had more time to freaking read. I always thought those emotions were so exaggerated. No way could what happens in a romance novel actually occur in real life.

But I'm feeling it. Right now. With Matthew DeLuca. And the way he's looking at me almost makes me think he might be feeling it too.

"So um, h-how have I been driving you crazy?" I swallow hard. I sound like a stuttering idiot, and I'm trying to calm my racing heart but it's no use. We're staring at each other in silence, the only sound our accelerated breathing, and then he reaches out. Rests his fingers against my cheek. Lets them drift along my face.

Slowly I close my eyes and part my lips, sharp pleasure piercing through me at his intimate touch. I curl my fingers against the wall as if I can grab onto it, afraid I might slide to the ground if I don't get a grip and soon. I can smell him. Feel him. We've been close to each other before, but not like this. Never like this.

"You look so damn beautiful tonight," he whispers, his rough voice sending a scatter of goose bumps across my skin.

"Thank you." I crack open my eyes to find he's moved even closer, one hand braced against the wall, the other still touching my face. Tilting my head back, I meet his gaze, my lids flickering when he strokes his thumb across my lower lip.

"It's taking everything inside of me not to just give in and kiss you," he admits gruffly, his hot eyes roaming over my face, then dropping lower, settling on my chest. I can feel my nipples tighten beneath the silk fabric of my dress and I'm suddenly, achingly aware of what little clothing I'm wearing. No bra, no panties . . .

My dress is the only barrier between Matt's hands and my skin.

"What's stopping you?" I reach out, slip my fingers down the length of his black tie. I can't believe I just said that. I can't believe I'm touching him, though really I'm only caressing his tie. Big deal.

But I can feel all that hot, hard strength beneath his shirt, the beat of his heart, the scent of his skin. Relief floods me. We've been dancing around this attraction for months and it feels like we're finally giving in. Well, I've been dancing around it. He always seemed mostly oblivious to me.

Maybe he isn't. If his current behavior is any indication, he definitely isn't.

"*I'm* stopping me. Or at least I should be," he says, resting both of his hands on my waist as he steps so close, our legs tangle, our chests brush. I hold my breath, waiting for what I know will be a totally disappointing answer.

He doesn't answer at all. Instead, he lowers his head, his mouth settling on mine, softly. Sweetly. His kiss obliterates everything, all of my thoughts, until I'm consumed with the sound and the feel and the smell of him. He surrounds me, consumes me, and when he thrusts his tongue deep inside my mouth, I'm lost.

And only Matt will be able to find me.

About the Author

New York Times and *USA Today* bestselling author MONICA MURPHY is a native Californian who lives in the foothills below Yosemite. A wife and mother of three, she writes new adult and contemporary romance. Visit her online at www.monicamurphyauthor.com and on Facebook at www.facebook.com/MonicaMurphyAuthor.

Visit www.AuthorTracker.com for exclusive information on your favorite HarperCollins authors.

Give in to your impulses . . .
Read on for a sneak peek at four brand-new
e-book original tales of romance
from Avon Books.
Available now wherever e-books are sold.

RESCUED BY A STRANGER
By Lizbeth Selvig

CHASING MORGAN
BOOK FOUR: THE HUNTED SERIES
By Jennifer Ryan

THROWING HEAT
A DIAMONDS AND DUGOUTS NOVEL
By Jennifer Seasons

PRIVATE RESEARCH
AN EROTIC NOVELLA
By Sabrina Darby

An Excerpt from

RESCUED BY A STRANGER

by Lizbeth Selvig

When a stranger arrives in town on a vintage motorcycle, Jill Carpenter has no idea her life is about to change forever. She never expected that her own personal knight in shining armor would be an incredibly charming and handsome southern man—but one with a deep secret. When Jill's dreams of becoming an Olympic equestrian start coming true, Chase's past finally returns to haunt him. Can they get beyond dreams to find the love that will rescue their two hearts? Find out in the follow-up to *The Rancher and the Rock Star*.

"Angel?" Jill called. "C'mon, girl. Let's go get you something to eat." She'd responded to her new name all evening. Jill frowned.

Chase gave a soft, staccato, dog-calling whistle. Angel stuck her head out from a stall a third of the way down the aisle. "There she is. C'mon, girl."

Angel disappeared into the stall.

"Weird," Jill said, heading down the aisle.

At the door to a freshly bedded empty stall, they found Angel curled beside a mound of sweet, fragrant hay, staring up as if expecting them.

"Silly girl," Jill said. "You don't have to stay here. We're taking you home. Come."

Angel didn't budge. She rested her head between her paws and gazed through raised doggy brows. Chase led the way into the stall. "Everything all right, pup?" He stroked her head.

Jill reached for the dog, too, and her hand landed on Chase's. They both froze. Slowly he rotated his palm and wove his fingers through hers. The few minor fireworks she'd felt in the car earlier were nothing compared to the explosion now detonating up her arm and down her back.

"I've been trying to avoid this since I got off that dang horse." His voice cracked into a low whisper.

"Why?"

He stood and pulled her to her feet. "Because I am not a guy someone as young and good as you are should let do this."

"You've saved my life and rescued a dog. Are you trying to tell me I should be *worried* about you?"

She touched his face, bold enough in the dark to do what light had made her too shy to try.

"Maybe."

The hard, smooth fingertips of his free hand slid inexorably up her forearm and covered the hand on his cheek. Drawing it down to his side, he pulled her whole body close, and the little twister of excitement in her stomach burst into a thousand quicksilver thrills. Her eyelids slipped closed, and his next question touched them in warm puffs of breath.

"If I were to kiss you right now, would it be too soon?"

Her eyes flew open, and she searched his shadowy gaze, incredulous. "You're asking permission? Who does that?"

"Seemed like the right thing."

"Well, permission granted. Now hush."

She freed her hands, placed them on his cheeks, roughened with beard stubble, and rose on tiptoe to meet his mouth while he gripped the back of her head.

The soft kiss nearly knocked her breathless. Chase dropped more hot kisses on each corner of her mouth and down her chin, feathered her nose and her cheeks, and finally returned to her mouth. Again and again he plied her bottom lip with his teeth, stunning her with his insistent exploration. The pressure of his lips and the clean, masculine scent of his skin took away her equilibrium. She could only follow the motions of his head and revel in the heat stoking the fire in her belly.

He pulled away at last and pressed parted lips to her forehead.

An Excerpt from

CHASING MORGAN
Book Four: The Hunted Series
by Jennifer Ryan

Morgan Standish can see things other people can't. She can see the past and future. These hidden gifts have prevented her from getting close to anyone—except FBI agent Tyler Reed. Morgan is connected to him in a way even she can't explain. She's solved several cases for him in the past, but will her gifts be enough to bring down a serial killer whose ultimate goal is to kill her? Find out in Book Four of The Hunted Series.

Morgan's fingers flew across the laptop keyboard propped on her knees. She took a deep breath, cleared her mind, and looked out past her pink-painted toes resting on the railing and across her yard to the densely wooded area at the edge of her property. Her mind's eye found her guest winding his way through the trees. She still had time before Jack stepped out of the woods separating her land from his. She couldn't wait to meet him.

Images, knowings, they just came to her. She'd accepted that part of herself a long time ago. As she got older, she'd learned to use her gift to seek out answers.

She finished her buy-and-sell orders and switched from her day trading page to check her psychic website and read the questions submitted by customers. She answered several quickly, letting the others settle in her mind until the answers came to her.

One stood out. The innocuous question about getting a job held an eerie vibe.

The familiar strange pulsation came over her. The world disappeared, as though a door had slammed on reality. The images came to her like hammer blows, one right after the other, and she took the onslaught, knowing something important needed to be seen and understood.

An older woman lying in a bed, hooked up to a machine feeding her medication. Frail and ill, she had translucent skin and dark circles marring her tortured eyes. Her pain washed over Morgan like a tsunami.

The woman yelled at someone, her face contorted into something mean and hateful. An unhappy woman—one who'd spent her whole life blaming others and trying to make them as miserable as she was.

A pristine white pillow floating down, inciting panic, amplified to terror when it covered the woman's face, her frail body swallowed by the sheets.

Morgan had an overwhelming feeling of suffocation.

The woman tried desperately to suck in a breath, but couldn't. Unable to move her lethargic limbs, she lay petrified and helpless under his unyielding hands. Lights flashed on her closed eyelids.

Death came calling.

A man stood next to the bed, holding the pillow like a shield. His mouth opened on a contorted, evil, hysterical laugh that rang in her ears and made her skin crawl. She squeezed her eyes closed to blot out his malevolent image and thoughts.

Murderer!

The word rang in her head as the terrifying emotions overtook her.

Morgan threw up a wall in her mind, blocking the cascade of disturbing pictures and feelings. She took several deep breaths and concentrated on the white roses growing in profusion just below the porch railing. Their sweet fragrance filled the air. With every breath, she centered herself and found her inner calm, pushing out the anger and rage left over from the vision. Her body felt like a lead weight, lightening as her energy came back. The drowsiness faded with each new breath. She'd be fine in a few minutes.

The man on horseback emerged from the trees, coming toward her home. Her guest had arrived.

Focused on the computer screen, she slowly and meticulously typed her answer to the man who had asked about a job and inadvertently opened himself up to telling her who he really was at heart.

She replied simply:

You'll get the job, but you can't hide from what you did.

You need help. Turn yourself in to the police.

An Excerpt from

THROWING HEAT
A Diamonds and Dugouts Novel
by Jennifer Seasons

Nightclub manager Leslie Cutter has never been one to back down from a bet. So when Peter Kowalskin, pitcher for the Denver Rush baseball team, bets her that she can't keep her hands off of him, she's not about to let the arrogant, gorgeous playboy win. But as things heat up, this combustible pair will have to decide just how much they're willing to wager on one another . . . and on a future that just might last forever.

"Is there something you want?" he demanded with a raised eyebrow, amused at being able to throw her words right back at her.

"You wish," Leslie retorted and tossed him a dismissive glance. Only he caught the gleam of interest in her eyes and knew her for the liar that she was.

Peter took a step toward her, closing the gap by a good foot until only an arm's reach separated them. He leaned forward and caged her in by placing a hand on each armrest of her chair. Her eyes widened the tiniest bit, but she held her ground.

"I wish many, many things."

"Really?" she questioned and shifted slightly away from him in her chair. "Such as what?"

Peter couldn't help noticing that her breathing had gone

shallow. How about that? "I wish to win the World Series this season." It would be a hell of a way to go out.

Her gaze landed on his mouth and flicked away. "Boring."

Humor sparked inside him at that, and he chuckled. "You want exciting?"

She shrugged. "Why not? Amuse me."

That worked for him. Hell yeah. If she didn't watch herself, he was going to excite the pants right off of her.

Just excitement, arousal, and sexual pleasure. That was what he was looking for this time around. And it was going to be fun leading her up to it.

But if he wanted her there, then he had to start.

Pushing until he'd tipped her chair back and only the balls of her feet were on the desk, her painted toes curling for a grip, Peter lowered his head until his mouth was against her ear. She smelled like coconut again, and his gut went tight.

"I wish I had you bent over this desk right here with your hot bare ass in the air."

She made a small sound in her throat and replied, "Less boring."

Peter grinned. Christ, the woman was tough. "Do you remember what I did to you that night in Miami? The thing that made you come hard, twice—one on top of the other?" He sure as hell did. It had involved his tongue, his fingers, and Leslie on all fours with her face buried in a pillow, moaning his name like she was begging for deliverance.

She tried to cover it, but he heard her quick intake of breath. "It wasn't that memorable."

Bullshit.

He slid a hand from the armrest and squeezed the top of her right leg, his thumb rubbing lazily back and forth on the skin of her inner thigh. Her muscles tensed, but she didn't pull away.

"Need a reminder?"

An Excerpt from

PRIVATE RESEARCH
An Erotic Novella
by Sabrina Darby

The last person Mina Cavallari expects to encounter in the depths of the National Archives while doing research on a thesis is Sebastian Graham, an outrageously sexy financial whiz. Sebastian is conducting a little research of his own into the history of what he thinks is just another London underworld myth, the fabled Harridan House. When he discovers that the private sex club still exists, he convinces Mina to join him on an odyssey into the intricacies of desire, pleasure, and, most surprisingly of all, love.

It was the most innocuous of sentences: "A cappuccino, please." Three words—without a verb to ground them, even. Yet, at the sound, my hand stilled mid-motion, my own paper coffee cup paused halfway between table and mouth. I looked over to the counter of the cafe. It was mid-afternoon, quieter than it had been when I'd come in earlier for a quick lunch, and only three people were in line behind the tall, slim-hipped, blond-haired man whose curve of shoulder and loose-limbed stance struck a chord in me as clearly as his voice.

Of course it couldn't be. In two years, surely, I had forgotten the exact tenor of his voice, was now confusing some other deep, posh English accent with his. Yet I watched the man, waited for him to turn around, as if there were any significant chance that in a city of eight million people, during the middle of the business day, I'd run into the one English acquaintance I had. At the National Archives, no less.

At the first glimpse of his profile, I sucked in my breath sharply, nearly dropping my coffee. Then he turned fully, looking around, likely for the counter with napkins and sugar. I watched his gaze pass over me and then snap back in recognition. I was both pleased and terrified. I'd come to London to put the past behind me, not to face down my demons. I'd been doing rather well these last months, but maybe this was part of some cosmic plan. As my time in England wound down, in order to move forward with my life, I had to come face to face with Sebastian Graham again.

"Mina!" He had an impressive way of making his voice heard across a room without shouting, and as he walked toward me, I put my cup down and stood, all too aware that while he looked like a fashionable professional about town, I still looked like a grad student––no makeup, hair pulled back in a ponytail, wearing jeans, sneakers, and a sweater.

"This is a pleasant surprise. Research for your dissertation? Anne Gracechurch, right?"

I nodded, bemused that he remembered a detail from what had surely been a throwaway conversation two years earlier. But of course I really shouldn't have been. Seb was brilliant, and brilliance wasn't the sort of thing that just faded away.

Neither, apparently, was his ability to make my pulse beat a bit faster or to tie up my tongue for a few seconds before I found my stride. He wasn't traditionally handsome, at least not in an American way. Too lean, too angular, hair receding a bit at the temples, and I was fairly certain he was now just shy of thirty. But I'd found him attractive from the first moment I'd met him.

I still did.

"That's right. What are you doing here? I mean, at the Archives."

"Ah." He shifted and smiled at me, and there was something about that smile that felt wicked and secretive. "A small genealogical project. Mind if I join you?"

I shook my head and sat back down. He pulled out his chair and sat, too, folding his long legs one over the other. Why was that sexy to me?

I focused on his face. He was pale. Much paler than he'd been in New Jersey, like he now spent most of his time indoors. Which should have been a turn-off. Yet, despite everything, I sat there imagining him in the kitchen of my apartment wearing nothing but boxer shorts. Apparently my memory was as good as his.

And I still remembered the crushing humiliation and disappointment of that last time we'd talked.